IN DUE TIME

JeNae LaShay

Copyright © 2020

All rights reserved. No part of this publication may be used or reproduced in any manner whatsoever without written permission except by a reviewer who may quote a brief passage.

Self-Published 2020

ISBN: 9798629339175

Edited by Em and a Pen

Dedication

To my parents: Mom, your support and silent strength never go unnoticed, you inspire me always. Dad, thank you for being a father and setting the bar high, may your spirit live through these pages.

To Machoman (W.Marc.): Thank you for holding me accountable. This work would never have seen the light of day without you.

Chapter 1
A Quarter Past Eight in the Evening

It has been a rough year, correction make that a rough four years for Shar. She ended a long-term relationship with 'Mr. Wrong', who was packaged as 'Mr. Right', a little over a year ago. Even though she vowed to let love bedazzle everyone else who may be interested and leave her alone, she couldn't resist the persistence of her know-it-all best friend Maniya, who set her up on a blind date.

Maniya knew that Dexter had taken Shar for a stressful, heart-wrenching ride that she didn't deserve. More importantly, she knew that Shar has always wanted to settle down with a great guy, marry him, and start a family. She felt partially responsible for Shar's love scar, because if it wasn't for her, Shar and Dexter never would have met. She just had to introduce her best friend to her man's best friend. Her intentions were great, however, much more was required.

Despite Shar's plea that she could never blame Maniya for what had happened, Maniya couldn't let that poor choice stain her friendship and she was determined to rectify the situation. If that meant screening men to help Shar find the love she deserved, then so be it.

The text message read:

*Sharrrr!!! Girl drop everything I have found the one. Yessss, everything that you want and then some! Be to **The Spot** tonight at 8:30, he's picking the show. Oh yeah and wear your tropical jumpsuit. Enjoy!*

Ordinarily, Shar would've just declined but after a day like today, she thought, "Why the hell not?"

So, there she was, pacing slowly from one side of the theatre to the other, glancing at the glass doors and thinking to herself:

"Why did I let that child talk me into this? I can't be that desperate, can I? What's taking him so damn long anyway?"

She was trying to keep her cool, but she was nervous. Since she split with Dexter, she couldn't bring herself to make a date and certainly a blind date was out of the question.

"Get yourself together missy," she thought, "If Maniya lied about him looking good and being qualified for the role, I'll just have to go."

Shar realized she was a little early, so she calmed down, leaned against the wall, and let out a gentle sigh. At that moment, she allowed herself to let go and think of the possibilities. Just as she pictured herself on a beach gazing at the ocean, a tall man walked up to her from behind and laid his hand gently on her shoulder. A little startled, she turned around to find her chocolate dream standing before her in linen pants, a baby blue cashmere sweater, and killer saddle leather shoes.

Mounds of caramel milk chocolate built this well sculpted masculine body that stood just over 6 feet. He had a smile that could make a desert moist. His hair was cut low with tapering around the edges, and his goatee danced around his full, luscious lips that rested lightly on his chin. His eyebrows and lashes were just enough to highlight his sharp sheer, gold shaded eyes.

Hell, his stare alone had the power to bring a strong woman to her knees. The physical aspects of Shar's chocolate dream was standing in front of her, and if his mental and emotional traits matched, she just might need the paramedics.

"You're Shar, right? I'm Stephan," he said with this smooth, deep voice. She gazed into his eyes as if she had been hypnotized. It took everything in her power to keep her legs from buckling.

"I'm sorry," she gasped.

"You're Maniya's friend, Shar, right?"

"Oh yes, accept my apologies please. You had me captivated. I mean you startled me for a moment."

"No, allow me. Look at you, you're shaking."

"I'm OK, really."

"I didn't mean to catch you off guard. Maniya told me that if I saw a beautiful ebony woman with a jumpsuit on that made me want to go to the islands, it would be you."

"Really, well I'm glad you spotted me. It's a pleasure to meet you Stephan." She attempted to extend her arm to shake his hand, but he went in for a hug instead. She could have melted on the spot. This fine specimen of a man smelled like a great mixture of rich amber and sandalwood, sweet, yet masculine, and his muscles filled his baby blue cashmere sweater like there was no tomorrow. She could damn near follow the chocolate brick road through the sweater.

"Damn," Shar thought.

She managed to keep her composure and broke away easily, yet reluctantly, from the hug and managed to ask, "So what are we going to see?"

"I thought a nice action movie would be good to watch, but it was sold out. So, *Tales from the Crypt* it is."

"*Tales from the Crypt*, like the television show from the 80s?"

"Yeah, that's it. They recreated it for the big screen. I hope you don't mind a horror flick."

"No, I don't mind."

"That's good, but if you get scared I'll be there to protect you."

To be honest, Shar was a little nervous, because this show used to terrify her as a kid. A year ago, she would've suggested going bowling or something instead, but today she's trying to face her fears and do something different. In the back of her mind, however, she knew that when she got home, all of the lights would be on. She'd even check to make sure the doors and windows were locked, and the garage door was down three or four times before laying down. On the other hand, there was something different about tonight. Stephan made her feel at ease and that was comforting.

They took each other's hand, walked toward the back of the theatre, and continued along with a general conversation about their days. The refreshment ads were rolling on the screen and the smell of popcorn intensified as they approached their seats.

"My apologies," Stephan whispered, "Do you want anything to eat or drink?"

"No, I'd rather not. I'm fine, but if you want something please get it."

"No, I'm good too. I was thinking that we could walk to the little café on the corner afterwards for some coffee or tea and conversation."

"That sounds great."

As they took their seats, the lights began to dim. Shar took a deep breath and placed her hands on her stomach. "Lord, what in the world am I getting myself into?" she thought.

"I heard this is really suspenseful, are you ready?"

"I guess."

"Do you like scary movies?"

"Not really."

"Oh no," he said sincerely. "Why didn't you tell me? We could have seen something else."

"It's okay, really. I feel safe with you," she said with a look of surprise after those words unintentionally escaped her mouth.

Some people in the audience began to make shhhhh sounds. Shar and Stephan looked at each other, grinned, and slid down to a level of comfort in their seats.

If tonight was any indication of the possibilities that existed for them, Shar couldn't be more intrigued.

Ding. Ding. Ding.

"Passengers, please return your seats to their upright positions and buckle your seat belts. We are preparing for landing at LaGuardia Airport. For those of you who are departing flight 777, please enjoy your stay in New York and for those of you who are continuing to Maine, we'll be back in the air momentarily. Thank you for flying with Skylines."

Shar slowly opened her eyes and looked around. There was no sight of that chocolate dream. She wondered, "Wait a minute. That felt too real to be a dream, are you kidding me? Just my luck. Why does it have to be too good to be true for me?"

The 757 Boeing was landing, and what a smooth transition it was too. Shar needed something to take her mind off her dream and fall back into a disappointing reality. "Yes, this pilot knows what he's doing. God thank you for another safe flight," she whispered.

When the seatbelt lights dimmed, Shar stood up, grabbed her belongings from the stowaway area, and waited to exit the plane. She had a look on her face that was screaming confusion. She was trying to figure out how she had a dream so vivid about a man that seemed so perfect for her. So, she wondered, if he could appear in her dreams, would he eventually appear in reality?

"It sure would be nice to meet Stephan for real," she thought, followed by a long sigh as she exited the boarding tunnel.

"Sharrrr," belted Maniya when she saw Shar walking towards her. She ran to her and gave the biggest hug that only great childhood friends could give.

"Oh, my goodness, it has been too long girl. I am so glad you're here."

"Me toooo!"

"Awwwww," they both exhaled as they stepped back and looked at each other.

"Welcome to New York chica, we are about to get this party started honey."

Shar and Maniya grew up in the same hometown just outside of Orlando in Eatonville, Florida. They lived three houses down from each other and became the sisters they never had. They went to school together through their college years; let's just say they are proud Seminoles. After they graduated from college, Shar accepted a position in Palm Coast, Florida as a Residential Coordinator for a prime senior living facility, and Maniya moved to New York to manage a modeling agency.

They both chose demanding careers, but they vowed to never go more than a year without seeing each other. Thus far, four years have passed, and their vows are still intact. Two ambitious, beautiful young ladies with brilliant minds and spirits, journeying through life realizing that it was different from what they used to talk about when they we're younger, laying beneath the enormous oak tree in Shar's backyard.

"Girl you are not going to believe the dream I had on the flight," snared Shar while Maniya was hailing a taxi.

"Really, what happened?" The taxi pulled up and the ladies entered. "Where to?" "1214 5th Ave.," Maniya replied.

"You know how we used to talk about our dream man when we were kids?" Maniya gave an affirming nod with overwhelming interest for more information. "Well, child, I met mine in this dream and you made it happen."

"I made it happen?"

"Yes, through a blind date at that."

"Get out of here, you hate those things."

"I know right, but man it felt so real. He was everything, I mean, everything I have ever described that I wanted in a man."

"I'm listening."

"Caramel milk chocolate complexion, over six feet tall, a smile that would make your heart melt and a voice that, ooh lord. I tried to close my eyes and go back," she said letting out a light laugh. Maniya started fanning Shar with her hands. "Woo, from what you are telling me honey, I don't blame you. I'm trying to close my eyes and go back with you to see him for myself." They both laughed and screamed so loudly while hi-fiving each other, the taxi driver slammed on the brakes and asked them if they were OK.

"We're fine, we're fine," Maniya said calmly after recovering from her brief laughing spell.

"From your response to my dream, I gather your desert is just as dry as mine?"

"Girl, at least you still have hope, I think I have thrown in the towel."

"Trust me, I'm almost there with you but if there is just a glimmer of hope that Mr. Right-full-circle is out there for me, we will connect eventually. Lord knows I have kissed enough frogs but instead of turning into my charming prince, they became toads."

"See what I'm saying," added Maniya with disgust as the taxi was coming to a halt in front of her building, "why bother?"

"She gave the driver a $50 bill. Shar grabbed her bags and they made their way inside the building. "Oh my God girl, this is really nice."

"Huge improvement from my first place, huh?"

"Most definitely, hell, we had to sleep with one eye open and both of our ears plugged. There was no telling what bug or rodent was going to try to attack us," said Shar as she plopped down on the sofa. Indeed, the hardwood floors, sleek furniture, and magnificent view of the city were truly an improvement. They laughed, sighed, and smiled while taking it all in. They both thought to themselves simultaneously how they have transformed from two little, shy country-bumpkins into two bold, brilliant bodacious women, on the move and making things happen.

Shar yawned and stretched her legs and arms out endlessly.

"Oh no my sister, you know damn well you are in the city that never sleeps. Yawning is not permitted."

"Really, chic?"

"Yes, really. We have about a good hour to find something fabulicious to throw on, shower, doll up and go party. Heyyyy!!!"

"Lord, what have I gotten myself into,' muttered Shar under her breath as she stood up.

"Besides, you just might meet your chocolate dream," said Maniya with a light chuckle as she trudged Shar along.

Chapter 2

11:45pm

The plan was to show Shar a great time during her stay, and Maniya was going to do just that. She wanted Shar to experience all of the flavors "The Big Apple" had to offer. Now, how everyone knows that Rome wasn't built in one day but Maniya, was anyone's guess.

"Wow, it is so beautiful out here. It feels like the Arctic is dancing with a summer breeze. It feels so good." Shar sighed as she took in the scenery while taking notice of the city lights and busyness of the street. The fact that it was almost midnight she belted out, "This is crazy, and I love it." Yes, she had a Hakeem moment from <u>Coming to America</u>, only no one shouted any obscene language in response to her adornment.

"Shar?"

"I'm out on the balcony."

Maniya joined her with a bottle of champagne and two flutes. She popped the bottle and poured them both some bubbly.

"Oh my goodness, I'm so glad you are here chic," she said, "We have to make a toast before we step out tonight."

"Yesssss," Shar agreed with excitement.

The ladies raised their glasses and Shar began the toast.

"Here's to living our lives with family, zest, success, and no stress."

"Yes, and let's not forget your true love and happiness," added Maniya.

"I know right? Aunt B said it best, didn't she?"

"In due time," they said in unison as they smiled and tapped their glasses.

Aunt B was the godmother of the neighborhood and all the kids gathered and played at her house. Her home was their home away from home and she treated them all like family. She was like an auntie to them, so they called her Aunt B.

"Awwww, I miss her," cried Maniya.

"I know right. Ok let's not, not right now."

The ladies chugged the champagne down, grabbed their purses, and headed out for a night to remember.

As they were about to exit Maniya's building, a pair of well-dressed gentlemen made it clear that chivalry was still very much alive.

"Allow me," he said.

As he opened the door, Shar and Maniya tilted their heads simultaneously while clutching their imaginary pearls with a quick upward glance at each other.

"Thank you," they said. Maniya stepped out the door and led the way to destination number one, which was the town car she reserved for the night.

"What in the world?"

"You know we have to be catered when we look like this."

"Hey, no complaints from me honey," said Shar. "If we are going to do it, then we are going to do it right."

The driver walked around the car to let them in.

"Good evening beautiful ladies. Where are we off to tonight?"

"M&M, please!" Maniya eagerly replied. No more country bumpkin town partying, because this Friday night is about to be all-the -way live missy. I want you to enjoy your stay and get your mind off of being lonely for a change."

"I'm all in lady."

It was the beginning of spring and these sisters were two of the fiercest flowers in the field. The dresses they wore fully accentuated their being. They looked as if they had just stepped off the cover of InStyle Magazine. When they walked, they commanded the room of those near and far and their Queen B peep toe heals made sure of it.

"What kind of club is M&M, Maniya?"

"You'll see soon enough. Just know that it is the prelude to the rest of the night."

"Rest of the night, you mean rest of the morning. How many clubs are you trying to hit exactly?"

"Relax Shar. You are in Manhattan baby, it's time to live a little and let lose." Maniya waved her arms, stuck out her tongue and screamed, "Heyyyyy!"

The car came to a halt and, moments later, the back door opened.

The driver extends his hand to assist Shar and Maniya out of the vehicle. Maniya gives him a tip and tells him to be out front for them in an hour. He tips his hat, smiles, and nods in response.

Shar looks around and makes an observation. "Um, where are all the men?" Maniya looks at her and smiles and responds, "Come on Shar."

It had been months since Shar allowed herself to indulge in the opposite sex, even as eye candy. So, she was in for a sweet treat tonight. None of the guys she worked with resembled anything she had fantasized about and when she wasn't working, she was home aside from quick runs to the store. To make matters worse, there wasn't much in Palm Coast anyway. If Shar was going to meet anyone who could hold her interest back home, it would truly be through divine intervention. Maniya, on the other hand, had her share of sweet treats and wasn't afraid to broadcast it.

Club M&M was boldly lit with neon pink and blue lights. A line of women wrapped the building, but Maniya and Shar did not have to wait, thanks to Maniya's VIP status.

"Well you asked where the men were, hmmh, hmmh, hmmmh," said Maniya as she cleared her throat. "Here they are."

"Oh my God," Shar whispered, "You brought me to a male strip …"

Before Shar could finish talking this hunk of dark chocolate, wrapped in a policeman's uniform, grabbed Shar by her waist and started winding his body against her while tilting backward. When he worked his way back upright, he positioned Shar's hand on his oiled chest and guided it up and around his neck.

"Oh…my…God, Maniya!"

"Get it Shar, damn girl."

"Girl, I need a drink," Shar said while holding back her panting breaths. "Thank you Mr. Officer." Shar let go of the well-oiled, ripped officer and grabbed Maniya's arm so she could stumble away in search of a bar.

"Girl you are so wrong for this. You know I haven't been around a man since I let Dexter go."

"Exactly, that's why I brought you here first."

"First?"

"Yes, first chic. It's time to live a little, let your hair down, and let loose," replied an enthusiastic Maniya.

A few steps later they made it to the bar. Shar leaned in to the bar and called out, "Two shots of Patron please."

She turned to Maniya and said, "Thank you sis, you always know what I need. I'm going to enjoy every minute of this."

"Two Patrons," said the bartender moments later.

The music was pumping loudly, very much in competition with hundreds of ladies screaming, laughing, and panting. Shar and Maniya raised their glasses, licked the salt from the rims, counted to three, and took their shot of Patron down like champs…followed by a few sucks on orange wedges. With their mouths twisted, they said, "Whewww," in unison and walked away towards a table while bobbing to the music with every step. There were fine pieces of chocolate wrapped delicately everywhere they turned; there was white chocolate, dark chocolate, and every mixture in between. While Shar tried to figure out which wrapper desired her attention the most, Maniya was getting her single bills ready to liven up the party.

"I love men in uniform."

"Well," Maniya said dragging her voice as she stood up waving bills in hopes of catching the attention of the barely dressed fireman, "You keep loving them in uniform and I'll keep loving them with nothing on at all."

"Wooooooo," she yelled, moving her body in a winding motion. A fireman worked his way over to her and managed to drop everything but his red-hot boxer briefs and hat along the way. He was called "The Extinguisher", and he was going to pump very hard to put out Maniya's fire.

Just as Maniya was getting hosed, the main lights went out, which left nothing but the stage and bar track lights illuminated. A siren noise began to echo through the room which was followed by a gentleman's voice.

"Ladies, ladies, laaddiieess! If you are in the building I want you to scream."

All the ladies in the building screamed to the top of their lungs.

"If you are having a great time tonight, say yeah."

"Yeahhh," shouted all the ladies!

"Now I know you can't see me right now," the voice continued, "But you can see this light moving around the room. Well now is not to time to be shy because one of you lucky ladies is about to be Mr. Anaconda's feast tonight. Oh yes, my, my, my. If the spotlight stops on you, please make your way to the stage and make yourself comfortable in my chair.

The spot light was moving about the room erratically with the fast pace of the music playing. As the music slowed down, so did the light. Within moments, the light stopped on Shar. In response, Maniya screamed louder than Shar.

"I'm not going up there."

"Yes you are, get up and go."

"Manny!"

"Go!"

A waitress brought over two shots of Patron, "These are from the DJ," she said.

"Right on time," Shar said nervously. She turned the glass up to her face and swallowed the Patron without salt or the orange wedge. She squinted her face and shook lose as if she was about to meet an opponent in a boxing ring. Shar made her way up to the stage and sat in the chair. Someone came up from behind her and placed a blindfold over her eyes.

"Oh my God," Shar moaned. The ladies in the audience could hardly contain themselves. They were more anxious than Shar was from screaming and making noises, wishing the light had stopped on them.

The music that was playing was very seductive when Mr. Anaconda slithered his way on the stage with his tongue out, moving up and down swiftly. Shar had no idea that this 6'4", smooth milk chocolate hunk, with long black locks, was at her feet making his tongue part his pearly whites to stroke his lips rapidly.

He spread her legs apart and moved upward, using his tongue to guide him. She tried to pull off the blindfold, but Mr. Anaconda grabbed her hands and placed them at the top of his head, guided them down his long locks around his neck, and down to his well sculpted pectorals. His skin felt like a tumbled stone wrapped in silk. Shar was trying to keep her composure, but there was a tingling sensation inside that she couldn't contain.

Mr. Anaconda straddled her, wrapped her arms around his waist, and began to take her on a joy ride. The crowd was going wild. As he grinded his sexy body against hers, he ran his fingers through Shar's hair and around her neck, and gently caressed her arms as he made his hands meet hers. He grabbed Shar's hands from his waist and guided them up to his chest then back down over his rippled abdominals, to the tip of his anaconda and beyond. When she reached the end of it, she knew how his name was derived.

"Sharrrr," yelled Maniya from the crowd. "Wooooooo, get it girl," she continued. Mr.

Anaconda stood up, took Shar by the hand, turned her around, bent her over and placed her hands on the seat of the chair. He grabbed her hips and positioned her ass in the perfect spot. He ran his hands down her spine and gave her ass cheeks a smack. The OMGs, 'Oohs' and 'Ahhs' from the spectators were louder than Shar's; but she contributed for sure. Mr. Anaconda looked out into the audience as he stroked Shar from behind, slithering his tongue rapidly. This man really knew how to entertain the ladies. Women were running to the stage throwing bills at his feet to show that he met their approval.

He leaned over to Shar and whispered in her ear, "Follow my lead, trust me." Shar nodded acceptingly and when she felt her legs being raised in the air, she wanted to retract, but it was too late.

Shar thought to herself, "I'm glad I didn't wear that dress."

Shar released a light giggle and continued to enjoy the ride. Anaconda had her legs on his shoulder and with one more lift from her waist, he used his head to spread her legs open and his mouth found his way to her pom pom. The ocean inside Shar's body had not been chartered in years, and there was about to be a tidal wave if this man didn't stop.

He paused for a moment, turned her around to face him and brought her back to standing position. He dropped down to the floor and slithered his body around and around until he worked himself back to Shar's feet. He put his arms around her legs and danced his way up to a standing position. He removed the blindfold from Shar's face, kissed her on the cheek and whispered sincerely, "Thank you."

Shar could barely stand up straight. The house lights came on and she made her way back to the table. Ladies were smiling at her and Maniya nearly knocked her over with a hug and a hi-five screaming, "Girlll!!!!! How was it, oh my God? As much as I come here I have never been up on that stage."

"I can't begin to explain everything I was feeling up there," said Shar as she tried to catch her breath. "I think I need another drink, wooh."

"Shoot, hold that thought Shar, we have to go. I told the driver to be out front at 1 o'clock."

Chapter 3

1:05 am

The ladies exited M&M laughing and smiling, and the driver was waiting for them as agreed. When they were in the car, Maniya told the driver to take them to Club Breezy. She knew that Shar would love this new hot reggae spot because Shar simply loved island music. Listening to it made her want to rock away in a hammock underneath a coconut tree.

"Maniya, girl after that ride on stage," Shar said as if she was out of breath, "I might need to stop by your place to freshen up." They both laughed and Maniya replied, "You'll be fine. If anything, you'll be sending signals to these men saying that it's drizzling down there right now. But, one of them might be lucky enough to bring on the thunderstorm, okay?"

"Maniya, you are a mess."

"I know, that's why you love me."

"OK, quick, let's do a mirror check. I know my hair is a hot mess."

"Shar you look great," Maniya said in between applying a fresh coat of lip gloss.

Shar rubbed her fingers through her hair, licked her lips and blew herself a kiss. The car came to a stop and the driver let them out.

"Last stop, Maniya said to the driver. We'll be out around 3:00."

She gave him another tip and they both sashayed into Club Breezy. The music was jumping, and this crowd definitely knew how to party. There were a lot of ladies there but, surprisingly, the men outnumbered them.

Shar was starting to think about changing residency as she surveyed the room. The ladies walked around to the beat of the music and scoped out the scene as they went along. There were two levels wrapped by bass with the DJ being in the center. The walls were covered with images of Reggae singers and beach scenes that looked as if you could jump in the water.

"Maniya," Shar said, "this place is really nice." "I think I'm in love."

"I knew you would love it, the DJ is great too. I hope your feet are ready because we are about to get down."

At that very moment, the DJ spun the record, as if he'd heard the magic words.

"Is that my song?" The music was bumping piercingly through the system.

"Beenie Man?"

"I'm drinking, I'm drinking …," belted the crowd as they sang along to the lyrics.

"Speaking of," said Maniya, "Let's go get a drink."

The ladies worked their way through the crowd with their arms up, dancing and singing along with the music until they made it to the bar.

"What can I get for you ladies?" the bartender called out.

"I'll have a Mangoberrita."

"Make that 2," Maniya added.

The music was going on continuously. With one hit after another, the crowd was enjoying every moment of it. Nearly everybody was moving to the music, one way or another. They were dancing on the floor together and alone, sitting and standing, bobbing their heads and tapping their feet. There were some people who were simply enjoying the company of others while others were watching and sipping on a mellow drink.

The bartender slid the ladies their drinks that were garnished with strawberries and orange slices. "The gentlemen at the end of the bar took care of these for you," said the bartender as he made a gesture to his left.

Shar and Maniya looked to their right and two guys lifted their drinks as if to salute and smile. The ladies returned the gesture, turned toward each other, and toasted, "May our great night continue."

"Yesssss!"

"Let's walk around Shar."

With their clutches under their arms and drinks in hand, the ladies strolled around the club to check out every angle, until they found a nice spot with enough elbow room to pause and enjoy the moment.

They watched people dance while they finished their drinks. The music was changing, and the ladies had just finished their drinks. At this point, they were looking for a table to place the empty glasses.

"We'll take those if we can have this dance," said one of the men from the bar.

Shar and Maniya gave the men their glasses and welcomed them to rock away to sound of Beres Hammond.

The men were nicely dressed and very gentleman-like. They took the ladies by the hand and led them to the dance floor. The music that was playing had a feel of palm trees swaying softly on a beach. So, it was only natural for their bodies to rock in that very motion, and they did. They twirled and danced the night away and their smiles and laughter were a sure giveaway of the enjoyment they shared. The ladies couldn't tell if the DJ had singled them out or not, but they did know that he kept playing one Beres Hammond hit after another. They must have danced through three songs straight and their dancing partners kept up with them every step of the way.

"Oh my God that felt really great, thank you," Shar whispered to her dance partner before they walked off the dance floor. "So, what's your name beautiful? I'm Ezekiel," he said.

"I'm Shar, pleased to meet you."

"The pleasure is all mine Shar. I hope you and your friend are enjoying yourselves."

"We are," Shar said. "It looks like they haven't had enough yet." They both laughed as they looked out to the dance floor and saw Maniya her dance partner still in the groove.

"Yeah, my brother Galvi is light on his feet."

"You're not bad yourself."

"Is that so?" "So are you new out here or have you simply been Manhattan's best kept secret?"

"No, I don't live here. I'm from down south. I'm just here visiting my girl for a few days."

"I see." "I would love to get to know you better if that's possible."

Maniya and Galvi were headed their way laughing and smiling.

"Wooo, I don't know the last time I've danced that much. It sure has been a while," Maniya said.

"Galvi, you OK brother? You look a little winded," Ezekiel said jokingly.

"Get out of here man."

"Well guys, we really had a great time but we have to get out of here."

"Hey Shar, how can I get in contact with you."

"I'm on Facebook, Shar Belle with an e," she replied as Maniya was ushering her out of Club Breezy.

"That was so much fun."

"It was but they were about to get clingy and want to go have coffee. Nope, not happening. I said we would be out of there by 3:00 A.M."

"Yeah, I don't think I would have lasted much longer myself."

As scheduled, the driver was waiting to take them to the next destination. Shar looked like she was ready to call it a night. Shar climbed in the car and let out a huge sigh as she kicked off her heels. Maniya waited for her turn and placed her hand on the driver's shoulder. She said, "Last stop, Nicky's Deli and then back to our starting point."

"You got it."

"Thanks, you're the best."

She got in the car and the driver closed the door behind her. Before he started the car, he thought the ladies might enjoy the starry night outside. So, he opened the moon roof and said, "The sky is beautiful tonight."

"It certainly is," they both replied, almost in unison as they plunged down a little deeper in the plush leather seats. Maniya decided to join Shar in the shoeless club as well.

"Maniya, girl I had a blast. What else is there for us to do? What's Nicky's?"

"Relax Shar, it's not a club. I just thought we danced our butt off, so it would only be right to top off the night with a nice fat slice of cheesecake."

"Cheesecake, after 3 in the morning?"

"Yesss honey, this is New York. Indulge while you can."

"We did dance our butts off, didn't we? What the hell, I'm in."

"That's my girl. Wait until you taste it. It's magnificent."

When the driver pulled up to Nicky's, Shar was asleep. But that didn't stop Maniya from sliding on her shoes and going into Nicky's to grab a slice of his infamous Cheesecake. She decided to get some fresh strawberries and blueberries on the side so they wouldn't feel too bad indulging in that thick piece of sin.

She made sure to grab two forks and some napkins, because there was no way that cake was going to make it back to her place without being touched first.

"Mmmmmmhh," she sighed as she sniffed the contents in the bag before heading back to the car. The smell of this cheesecake was going to wake Shar up for sure.

Maniya made her way back to the car and the driver was there waiting with the door ajar. She slid inside, kicked off her shoes once again, opened the bag from Nicky's, and waved it back and forth under Shar's nose.

Shar leaned her head to the left, stretched her arms upward and said softly, "Mmmmm, something smells heavenly." Maniya pulled the cheesecake from the bag, popped the lid of the box open and, before she knew it, she swiped the tip of the slice with her fingers. The cake on her finger tips quickly connected to her taste buds. She closed her eyes and leaned her head back against the seat and said," Ooh Shar, it tastes even better."

Shar was up now and she realized Maniya was eating with her fingers. "Really chic?"

"Girl I couldn't resist. I do have forks in the bag." Shar laughed at Maniya, grabbed the two forks and said, "Girl you are still crazy."

Maniya took her fork from Shar and they both plowed into the cheesecake. If the driver didn't know any better, he would have thought the two of them were going half on a baby with all of the moaning and groaning he heard.

"This cake is too damn good."

Just as the driver was pulling up to Maniya's building, they were finishing their last bite. Shar asked for a napkin and when Maniya reached in the bag for one she felt a small container. "Awww man, I got so carried away I forgot about the fruit." They laughed heavily while holding their stomachs.

"I don't think we would have had room for that if we wanted to. I'm stuffed," said Shar.

The ladies laughed a little more, grabbed a napkin and wiped away any remnants of the cheesecake. They slipped on their shoes, grabbed their belongings, and thanked the driver for his service.

"What a night," Shar said jovially as they walked into the building. "What a night." Maniya didn't reply with words but the expression on her face was confirmation that she agreed.

It didn't take long for them to get to Maniya's apartment. When they made it inside, neither of them made it passed the living room. They were out for the count within minutes of flopping down on the furniture.

Chapter 4

8:45 am

There was a tune of chimes coming from Shar's phone; she could hear it, but she wasn't able to see it with her eyes closed. She opened one eye and then the other. She released the pillow that she'd managed to hold on to throughout her sleep and wiped the little drool from her mouth. She'd almost forgotten where she was for a minute, until she scanned the room and saw Maniya dead to the world, sleeping on the chaise by the balcony.

Shar yawned and stretched, still trying to figure out where her phone was hiding. The tune was still playing, but why she still had her alarm set was beyond her. But if her phone had any idea of the night, she had just hours ago, it would stop making that noise. "Okay, okay," she said, agitated, as she got off the sofa. When she stood up, she could see that her purse did not make it to the sofa with her. Somehow, it fell behind it. She walked around to pick it up holding on to the sofa for mild support. Just as she reached inside to grab her phone, the alarm stopped. She took the phone out anyway and made sure that it didn't come on again until she needed it, the day she was catching a flight to go home.

She went to the kitchen to find some tea to start her morning right.

"I just know she has some tea in here somewhere," she said as she searched in the cabinets.

"Ahhh, a tea kettle, "the tea must be close," she hoped. Shar took the tea kettle from the cabinet, rinsed it out, filled it with water, and placed it on the stove. She had hoped to have found the tea before the water started to boil, or Maniya would have to wake up and tell her where it was. She was determined not to let this little hangover get the best of her.

She continued on her quest to look in drawer after drawer through the last of the cabinets, without any sign of tea. Meanwhile, Maniya began to toss and turn and mistook the sounds of the cabinets and drawers closing, as knocks at the door. Out of nowhere she asks, "Who is it, who is it?"

Shar replies, "Maniya, it's me, Shar." The teakettle started to whistle and Maniya's sleep was officially over.

"What in the hell," she said with her eyes now wide open. I could've sworn someone was knocking at my door. Shar, what are you doing?"

"I'm trying to make some tea, but I can't find any."

Maniya stretched and got up reluctantly. She walked over to the kitchen and said, "Did you look in the canister marked "Tea" by chance?" as she reached for the canister in front of Shar.

"Wow, really? If it was a snake it would have bitten me."

Maniya laughed at her and grabbed two cups from the cabinet and placed the tea bags inside.

"Oh my God, how much did we drink last night? My head hurts."

"It must've been the shots. Then again, the margarita wasn't weak."

As Shar poured the water in the cups she said, "I know one thing, I had a great time. What did you think about the guys at Club Breezy?"

"What guys? Oh yeah, they were nice, but I didn't even get the name of the one I danced with."

"Really? I think they were brothers. I can't say I remember his name or the one I was talking to. He was nice though. Maybe I should have given him my number, huh?"

"Who knows Shar, I told you how I feel about this relationship thing these days, besides, you are on Facebook."

"You're right, que sera sera." Shar sipped her tea and exhaled.

"Well, I know what won't be happening," Maniya added, "and that's us sitting around this place all day. We need to go downstairs to the gym and burn off some of that cheesecake before we do anything else."

Shar looked at Maniya as if she had lost her mind. But she knew she was right. "It's a good thing I packed some workout clothes," she thought. "Sounds good," Shar said.

They took their last sip of tea, freshened up, and got dressed for the gym.

"Shar are you ready?"

"Tying my shoes, I'll be out in a minute."

Maniya was waiting at the door when Shar came running out of the room. "Someone's ready for a workout, huh?"

"You know I'm always ready. I may look crazy at the thought at first, but I'd rather be healthy than lazy any day."

The ladies left the apartment, ready to go. "We can get water at the gym, management keeps it stocked."

"OK," Shar replied. "What kind of equipment do they have?"

"Girl they have some of everything. And yes, they have your elliptical."

"That's all I needed to know."

"Well don't get too comfortable on that, because I know this killer ab routine I want you to try," Maniya said as she waved her keyless tag over the panel for entry.

"Girl, this reminds me of our college days. We used to be workout fanatics."

"I still try to get at least three or four workouts in. But sometimes life happens."

"No kidding, same here. But guess what? We are still looking good and we are healthy."

"Yesss, thank God for that."

Maniya grabbed two hand towels from the shelf and two waters from the cooler before securing a clear area to stretch.

"Here Shar," she said giving her a water and towel. "Let's stretch before we get started."

They stretched for a few minutes, drank a little water, and headed for the cardio machine of their choice.

"Let's do cardio for about 30 minutes, and then we'll do that ab routine I was telling you about."

"Sounds good Manny."

"Manny? You haven't called me that in years, Shar."

Shar laughed a little and said, "I know right? See you in 30."

Manny was a nickname Shar gave Maniya when they were kids. It slipped out one day while playing in Aunt B's yard and she liked how it sounded so she stuck with it.

The 30 minutes on the machines flew by and the ladies started their ab routines.

"Manny, you didn't lie about this being a killer routine. My Lord!"

Maniya laughed and kept going. "You can do this 'Ms. Thang'. You know you like it when the men all pause in your presence."

"And you know it." Shar replied.

The ladies worked up a sweat and finished drinking their water. After cleaning off the equipment, they headed back to Maniya's apartment to shower and get ready for the remainder of the day.

Chapter 5

Noon

"Hello."

"What's up, E?"

"Hey Galvi man, what's going on? How are you feeling?"

"Nothing much man, just waking up really. I feel alright considering all the drinks we kicked back. You know what I mean?"

"Hey, I feel ya man. We didn't take it too easy at Club Breezy last night."

"Nah, we went in kinda hard."

"Well you know the crows weren't giving us a choice; it felt like the same ole, same ole until…"

"Oh here we go," Galvi interrupted, "until what?"

"Well until those beautiful ladies walked in."

"I knew you were about to say something about them."

"It's true. You know nothing else in there caught our eyes."

"Yeah, but."

"But what? We danced with them and had a great time."

"Yeah, that's it, in just that moment. I didn't even get the name of the chic I danced with."

"Well, that was your mistake. I got the name of the sweet brown sugar that graced me with her presence."

"Man, get out of here. You sound like you're in love already. You don't even know much about her."

"I know enough. She's gentle and smooth and down to earth and, on top of all of that, she's gorgeous."

"They were both pretty cool. Did you get her number though?"

"No, her friend was dragging her out of the club. She shouted out her last name, remember? She told me to look her up on Facebook."

"Hell nah, that's crazy. She must be married or involved with someone."

"I don't know man and, frankly, I don't care. If I find a window of opportunity to get to know her better I'm jumping in."

Galvi laughed at his brother and said, "Damn dude, what did she do to you on that dance floor?"

"She had some great moves but, if I'm being honest, her smile and those almond shaped eyes had my heart skipping a beat. I never have felt that before and it kind of caught me off guard."

"Get the hell out of here E. I'm gonna have to come over there and slap the rest of that liquor out of your system," said Galvi jokingly. "But on another note, are we still on for lunch today?"

"Yeah no doubt, a late lunch in the city."

"Cool, what's the name of that spot again?"

"DESTINY. It's knew and trending. I have to do a review on it, so I figured we could go there before we visit the Boys and Girls Club back in the neighborhood."

"Sounds good, I'll see you there about 2."

"Yo."

"Yo."

They ended their phone call and started getting ready.

Ezekiel and Galvi were the only children their parents had. Their mother raised them alone after their father died in a train accident when they were pre-teens. They depended heavily on the Boys and Girls Club on their block, because their mom had to hold two jobs at times to keep things afloat. Seeing how she struggled day to day to make sure they had their necessities and desires, they made it a point to be successful and be in a position to give back to their mother and the BGC that helped raise them to be the men they'd become.

They took full advantage of the mentoring program the BGC offered, Ezekiel and Galvi finished high school at the top of their classes and accepted full scholarships to UPenn. Before they graduated with Financial

Management degrees, they ventured out and made great investments in their junior and senior year, which helped them launch the Family Business Financial Investment firm. They have managed to help thousands of small businesses and startup companies pave their way to success over the years. They never lost sight of the components that made it possible, God, their mom, and the BGC.

Their mom couldn't be prouder of them for enabling her to retire early and travel the world and give back to the community that helped fill the gap of their father's absence. Her only wish that hasn't been fulfilled yet is for the two of them to find someone to love who would love them in return and start a family.

Ezekiel was ready for that chapter of his life, but Galvi wasn't certain that he was marriage material. Unlike Ezekiel, Galvi likes multiple women because he doesn't want to get too attached to one. He's not sure why he feels this way, but he believes part of the reason stems from losing his father at a young age. Ezekiel used his father's love to love others. Even though he has been hurt in the past, he still has hope of finding that special someone to spend his life with. A voice inside of him has always whispered, "In due time, it will all come together." He has faith that it's going to happen.

Chapter 6

12:15 pm

"Maniya," Shar called out as she entered the living room, looking radiant in her flowing summer dress.

"I'm out here," Maniya replied from the balcony. Shar walked outside on the balcony to join her.

"Hey beautiful, I love that color on you."

"You do? I wasn't too sure about it."

"Blue has always been your color, and that Royal blue is popping Manny."

"Maybe it's this jumper that's throwing it off for me."

"Girl, please, you look amazing. Do I need to go grab a mirror?"

Maniya gave Shar a smirk and smiled. She knew she looked good, but she enjoyed hearing others say it sometimes.

"Shar, you know how I am sometimes. I'm fine. You look great, too. Where did you get that dress?"

"Chile, thank you," she said as she took a small twirl. "I got this dress from one of those catalogs. You know me, I've had it for years."

"Well, it looks very nice; you're giving the beautiful turquoise waters of the world some fierce competition."

"Thanks bestie. So what are we about to get ourselves into today?"

"I figured we'd take it easy after that workout this morning."

"Ya think?"

"Yeah, we are going to a few shops and then we'll get a bite to eat at this new spot around the way."

"Sounds good, my stomach is trying to tell me something already," Shar said with one hand on her belly while trying to silence the growl.

Maniya laughed lightly, "I know right? Mine is too, but let's grab a granola bar to hold us over for now. I hear this place we're going to has some great food."

"OK. What type of restaurant is it? I hope it's not one of those bougie spots, because I'm going to need more to fill me up than a piece of grass, a slice of meat, and fruit shavings."

Maniya could not hold her laughter. "Girl, you are too much. It's a little high end, but I hear the top chef likes his food to be tasted and he's quite generous."

"Good. Well I'm ready when you are."

"OK give me a second," said Maniya as she pulled out her ringing cell phone from her purse.

"Hello?"

"Maniya?"

"Who wants to know?"

"Wow, has it been that long, you don't recognize my voice?"

"Uh, who is this?"

"Baby, it's me, Deran."

Maniya looked startled and she nearly dropped her phone when she heard the name, but she managed to get herself together before too much time had passed.

"Deran," she said.

"Yes baby, how are you? How have you been? Oh my God, you don't know how much I've anticipated this moment, talking to you again. I'm sorry, let me stop rambling. Hello?"

"I'm here."

"So say something, are you happy to hear from me, I mean what? I know it's been a few years since we've talked."

"You're right; it has been a few years now, and I thought I made it clear then that we had nothing else to talk about."

"Baby please, can you just hear me out? I miss you so much, baby, you just don't understand."

"No, I think I do. I'm not trying to be harsh, because Lord knows I'm not. I just want to keep things 100 and, right now, I don't have the time, or the energy, to give to you right now Deran, I don't."

"Maniya, baby, I wanna see you. I'm in New York for a few days and I wanna see you. Can you please just grant me that?"

"Deran I have to go, I can't promise you that."

"Just tell me you'll think about it at least and I'll call you tomorrow."

Maniya sighed deeply and ended the call.

"Maniya, I hope that wasn't who I think it was."

Maniya looked at Shar with a near deadly facial expression. "Honey, the devil is busy. But I'm not going to let him steal my joy."

"What does he want after all this time and his treasure trove of lies?"

"Who are you asking? Ahhh, something told me not to answer that call. Wow, it's just a little pass noon, and I feel like I need a drink after that encounter."

"I don't believe he had the nerve to call you up after years with no contact."

"Okayyyyy and especially after our engagement disaster."

"After all of those years with him!"

"4 going on 5, only to find out he was married to someone else that already had his child that he claimed he couldn't wait for me to have—Ooh Lord," Maniya said angrily, looking as if she could strangle someone.

"I know Manny, but it's OK, you got through it. You look beautiful, you're healthy, and you are successful. He didn't break you."

"Why does he think I should see him just because he's in New York for a few days? I don't owe him any of my time. The audacity…"

"You're so right about that."

"I forgave him for his actions and moved on."

"I know Manny, but have you told him that?"

"Should I have to?"

"Maybe."

"Really Shar?"

"Well, at least you'd know there is complete closure and, no matter what his agenda is, you can walk away feeling great knowing that all of that pain and confusion is behind you."

"I don't know. I have to think about it, but not right now. Come on, let's go, the car should be out front waiting."

The ladies grabbed their purses and granola bars off the counter and headed out the door. The driver from last night was waiting for them patiently when they exited the building. He greeted them with a smile and an open door. "Good Afternoon," they both said as they entered the car. He tilted his head down, replying nonverbally, and closed the door behind them.

"Where are you beautiful ladies going today?"

"New District please," Maniya replied.

"In the mood for a little shopping I see."

"Yeah, we're going to peruse a little."

"Sounds like fun," the driver said as he began his route.

"Hey Manny, did you make a reservation for us at that restaurant?"

"Nah, I don't think I need to. It's the middle of the afternoon, so we should be good."

"OK, the way you talked earlier made it seem like it's a popular place."

"Well, it is, people have been tagging it like crazy. I've heard nothing but great things about it."

"I can't wait to check it out."

"I know right?"

"So have you given anymore thought to what's his face?"

Maniya released a deep sigh and faced Shar, "I'm trying not to go there. You know how long it took for me to pull myself together after that ordeal with him?"

"I know but, like I said, meet up with him and just get that final closure. Maybe he needs to hear that you forgave him to let go of what could've been, you know?" Maniya exhaled heavily. "And, maybe, once you see him face to face and acknowledge your forgiveness, true love can come to you."

"Child, please, love may be for some people, but Maniya Alese Stetson has been there, done that, #not interested.com, next, hello."

"Lord have mercy on her soul please, this girl is crazy."

"Hmmmh, no I'm serious Shar, but enough of that. Don't let my feelings on love be a dark cloud over your dreams."

"I'm not. You know I understand where you're coming from, because love hasn't always been reciprocated to me either. But deep in my heart and soul I know it will happen. I don't want to give up on it, ya know?"

"Well, to be honest, I try not to think about it. I mean, I was so close to having it, or so I thought. Anyway, enough of talking about it, like I said before, this mess is not about to steal my joy. It's a beautiful day to be beautiful, happy, shop, and have some fun," said Maniya following it up with a big smile and a personal round of applause.

"I'm with you Manny, there's nothing to it but to do it."

"Alright ladies, New District awaits," said the driver as he pulled up to the front entrance of the mall.

"Wow, this mall makes the Millenia look like it was built in B.C."

"Shar stop, but you are right," said Maniya followed by a light laughter.

"Let's go chic, there's a new boutique in here I've been waiting to check out."

The ladies walked around the mall and window shopped mostly but managed to peruse around a few shops and purchase enough items to need assistance to the car.

"My God Manny, why did you let me buy all of this stuff?"

"Me? You were no better at helping me." They smiled and continued to walk to the car.

"Hey, we might as well enjoy the moment. Hell, there was a time when we had to invent our own convertible outfits, because we couldn't afford to go shopping."

"Okkaay!! Swapping tops and bottoms and rearranging color schemes."

"Yes ma'am, whatever it took. But, one thing about it was, 'We always looked good,' they said simultaneously as they faced each other before getting in the car.

"Wow, Manny. God has really brought us a long way."

"Two little girls with a dream."

"I know right, a dream that has pretty much become our reality."

"Amen."

"But, God!"

Zhamin was always punctual when he drove for Maniya's company, and he was consistent as her personal driver this weekend. He made their travels through the city seamless. After putting their bags in the trunk and making sure their door was closed, he entered the car and asked the ladies where they were heading next.

"We are starving Zhamin. I can't think of the name of this restaurant, but it's fairly new off of Hope Blvd."

"I know exactly where you're talking about, a lot of executives go there. I hear it's always nice."

"I know, so we're going to check it out."

"No problem, I'll have you there in no time."

"Thanks," said the ladies in harmony.

They made themselves comfortable by leaning their heads back and enjoying the ride. Shar was thinking to herself how she could get used to this chauffer treatment, while Maniya was dreading that phone call.

Chapter 7

2:30 pm

The streets were busy as always, but Zhamin managed to get the ladies to the restaurant within minutes. Shar wasn't used to this type of congestion on the streets. People were crowding sidewalks and cars were crowding lanes.

"Here we are ladies," Zhamin said as he drove across the pebbled horseshoe driveway to the restaurant. He placed the car in park and walked around to let the ladies out. Shar and Maniya were putting their glosses and powder puffs away after a minor touch up. They were ready to go. When they stepped out of the car, they were amazed at how beautiful this place was in daylight. They couldn't imagine how that beauty was magnified at night. The restaurant was huge; it took up the entire block. There were grand statues of Aphrodite, Eros, Artemis, Demeter and Zeus at guard in the front. The structure consisted of natural stones and marbled columns with greenery and lights accentuating them. Captivated by the outside appearance, the ladies couldn't wait to head inside.

They followed the flavorful aroma to the oversized glass doors with a cream marbled door handle that spelled DESTINY vertically. As the ladies approached the doorway, the glass doors began to slide open in the opposite direction, carrying the respectable letters to form DESTINY on both sides of the doorway while ajar.

"Wow, DESTINY, that's hot. Maniya, are you sure we can afford this?"

"Girl yes, that's what's so crazy about it. It's not cheap by a long shot but it's not for just the top elite either."

"It sure does look the part," whispered Shar.

Maniya nodded with a mild grin on her face as they walked in. The inside was a great complement to the casing of the restaurant.

All the natural colors of stone, water, and fire created a grand scene. It would be hard for anyone to enter or leave this place in a foul mood.

"This is beautiful and, may I say, the food smells great," said Maniya.

"That's for certain."

"Good afternoon ladies. My name is Asher. Welcome to DESTINY, we take pleasure in giving you a taste of what your future will hold. Will there be anyone else joining the two of you?"

"No," they said harmoniously.

"Wonderful, come with me."

With two golden scrolls in hand, Asher escorted the ladies to their table with a tri-colored waterfall in clear view.

"Here you are ladies," he said after making sure that they were seated comfortably. He gave them the golden scroll menus and told them to press the button on the side to release it and the arrows as they appear to go to the next page. Trying not to look too impressed, the ladies followed the instructions that were provided and glanced over the menus.

"Take a moment to look those over. I'm sure you will find whatever your heart desires."

"Thank you," said Shar before Asher walked away.

"Maniya, girl, is this place for real?"

"I know."

"He wasn't kidding about finding something our heart desired, because there's something tasteful representing all areas of the globe."

"Tell me about it, what are you going to get?"

"Let's get some stuffed mushrooms to start and we can look over the menu a little more."

"Okay."

Asher made his way back to the table with a golden pitcher filled with water. As he poured water in their glasses he said, "I hope the two of you have had enough time to look over the menu and found something delightful to start your meal."

"We have, thank you," said Shar,

"What can I get for you?"

"We're going to have some stuffed mushrooms and I would like a Sun-Kissed lemonade," she added.

"And I would like a whisky-sour with a splash of pineapple."

"Manny, really?" Shar asked slightly concerned.

"Yes, really."

"Got it. Can I get you two anything else?"

"Just a few more moments for us to decide on our meal please."

"Take your time. I will be back in a few moments with your drinks."

"Thank you," said Maniya.

"Manny, girl, you were serious about that drink huh?"

"I've been trying not to think about that phone call, but it's weighing on me. Maybe this drink will ease my mind a little."

"Do you still have feelings for him? I mean, do you still love Deran?"

"Don't play with me, Shar. Hell no, with everything he put me through... are you serious? I told you that love shit is overrated, and I am over it."

"I had to ask Manny, because you had a lot of time invested in him and your relationship. If you did, it would be understandable, ya know?"

Maniya looked across the table at Shar with laser eyes and said, "Do you know…"

Shar knew this was about to take a wrong turn. She took a deep breath and tried to brace herself for what was coming.

"Here you are ladies. A Sun-Kissed lemonade for the beautiful lady in turquoise and a whiskey-sour with a splash of pineapple for the beautiful lady in royal blue.

"Thank God," Shar said to herself when Asher appeared. They both said thank you and sipped their drinks.

"Ooh, this is heavenly. How's yours Manny?"

Maniya signaled 'OK' with her fingers as she went in for another taste. "Humph, it's just what the doctor ordered."

They laughed and glanced at the menus again.

"Okay Asher, I think we are ready to order now," said Shar.

"Wonderful, what does your heart desire?"

"I will have the Shrimp Divine with a house salad," said Shar.

"And I will have Cupid's Choice with asparagus and scalloped potatoes with the steak tips cooked at medium-well."

"Excellent. Let me get these menus out of your way and get these orders in. I'll have the stuffed mushrooms out in a few moments."

The ladies gave Asher their menus and took in the ambiance of DESTINY. The restaurant was quite busy for an afternoon, but the service was so impeccable that no one felt like there was much of a wait for anything. The bartenders worked painlessly to service the guests at the bar, and the waiters and waitresses were just as benevolent with the guests at the table.

With such great service, atmosphere, and from the smell of it, divine cuisine, there was no wonder this place was getting rave reviews that would take the restaurant industry to new heights.

Shar exhaled and smiled before asking Maniya how she was feeling. But, before she could, Asher was back at their table with stuffed mushrooms that smelled amazing.

"I hope I didn't take too long."

"Not at all," Shar replied.

"They smell delicious."

"Please enjoy," said Asher before walking away.

The removed the silverware from their napkins and placed a few mushrooms on the appetizer saucers.

"Man these things are smoking, we better let them cool off a minute," said Maniya.

"A minute is about all I have," said Shar. They both laughed and went in for a taste.

Their facial expressions said it all, but they made it a point to express how good those mushrooms tasted. They managed to exchange a little dialogue in between bites.

"Oh my God, I don't think I've tasted a stuffed mushroom like this before, or am I just hungry?"

"Nah, I think you're right. There can't be anything artificial in them."

They went in for another and took a sip of their drinks. It was clear that the ladies were really enjoying themselves as they took in the scenery, the mix of people, and the savory taste of their appetizer. What made it more amazing was the fact that they had only seen a small portion of what DESTINY had to offer.

Chapter 8

3:15 pm

"Galvi man, so, what do you think?"

"I must say I'm impressed, really. If the service stays like this and the food," he said as he rubbed his belly, "man, if they continue to deliver great cuisine, DESTINY will lead the restaurant industry."

"I know we went into business together for a reason. This place is a symbol of hope, and, I think, something we need today for people to feel good about themselves and others. It just exudes love to me for some reason."

"Man, how in the hell do we always get on this subject?"

"For someone who 'loves' himself more than life, you should welcome the mentioning of the word."

"Whatever E. Let me guess, now you're thinking of the young lady from last night, right?"

"Well since you brought her up," Ezekiel said followed by a grin on his face.

"Did you look her up on the book yet?"

"No, I'm hoping chance will have us face to face again."

"Good luck with that."

"Man, it is called faith and I believe it will happen," said Ezekiel as he reached for his drink.

Shar and Maniya were still admiring DESTINY and enjoying light conversation when Asher brought their entrees to the table.

"I have the Shrimp Divine for you," he said placing the dish in front of Shar, "and I have the Cupid's Choice for you. Be careful, the food is extremely hot. Is there anything else I can get for either of you?"

"My side salad," Shar reminded him.

"Yes, that's on its way out. Can I get you ladies something else to drink?"

"I'll have another Sun-Kissed lemonade."

"Make that two," said Maniya.

"You got it," Asher said. As he turned to walk away, another waiter had arrived with Shar's salad.

"Perfect. Here's your salad, sorry for the wait," said Asher.

"Thank you."

"Enjoy ladies."

Maniya and Shar blessed the meal before them and apologized for not blessing the mushrooms earlier, because the hunger pains got the best of them. The aroma alone from the food had them mesmerized. They wanted to compliment the chef for that alone, not to mention the display as well. Everything on their plate looked like a work of art. They took a few moments before taking a bite of anything and, when they did, silence won them over.

Maniya tried to hold back her thoughts, because she felt a little overwhelmed by the whole experience. It was as if the food had her whipped or something. She licked her lips and said, "Shar, if love could look as appetizing, smell as fragrant, and taste as heavenly as the food in this place, I'd be all over it."

"I thought it was just me, but if it has you mentioning the word love, then it must be incredible."

"I need to go to the restroom, but I don't want to leave the table."

Shar laughed and said, "Manny you better go. I won't eat your food, I promise."

Maniya got up from the table just as Asher returned with their drinks.

"Just who I needed to see, where is the restroom?"

Asher pointed to his right and said, "Go straight down and follow the curve of the bar, you'll see it on the right."

"Thank you."

"How is everything?" Asher asked.

"Absolutely wonderful, we are very impressed with DESTINY for sure," said Shar.

"We aim to make your experience pleasurable in hopes that you will take that pleasure with you and share it with someone else."

"That is so beautiful," Shar said blushingly.

"Is there anything else I may do for you?"

"No, we are fine for now, but we may need a few boxes. This is a lot of food."

Asher smiled and said, "Not a problem, I'll have some on stand-by for you."

"Wonderful. Thank you."

Maniya made her way around the bar and she had the restroom in sight. But that wasn't the only thing in clear view.

"Damn, maybe we were seated in the wrong place," she said as she connected the dots to the handsome men scattered on this side of the restaurant. She made eye contact with a few of them, nearly fumbling her way into the ladies room.

"Hey man, did you see the royalty gem that just passed us?"

"No, where?" asked Ezekiel as he looked around.

"She just passed us, and she was wearing that dress well."

"Fine time to ask me if I saw her, especially now when she is out of sight."

"Hey bruh, I just got a glance of her myself."

"Umhmh, tell me anything," said Ezekiel before picking up his glass to finish his drink.

"DESTINY is where it's at for sure."

Ezekiel was signaling the bartender for the check when Galvi said, "Hey man, here she comes."

As she got closer to them Ezekiel said, "She is beautiful but she looks familiar."

Maniya glanced over at the bar with a big smile on her face as she passed by.

"She doesn't look familiar to you G?"

"Not really."

"Isn't that the girl from Club Breezy that you were dancing with?"

"You think so? You know I was on a couple of Hen last night. I would hate to think I let her get passed me."

"I tried to tell you those girls were different but you weren't trying to hear me."

Maniya stepped lightly back to the table, but she couldn't wait to tell Shar about the pre-dessert treats she saw scattered on the other side of the restaurant, especially the two chocolate drops that were sitting at the bar.

"Whooh, I feel so much better," said Maniya as she checked her plate out to make sure Shar didn't take any of her juicy steak.

"Really Manny, I didn't bother your food," said Shar. "You came back just in time."

Maniya looked at her like she was crazy and Shar couldn't help but laugh. "I'm kidding, damn is it that good? I have to try it now." She reached over and stuck her fork in a piece of steak and Maniya allowed the transaction without a fuss.

"It's great, isn't it?"

"Mmmmm umhmh."

"Told you. Oh, I almost forgot. There are some good-looking men in here on the other side. Best of all, they are not with women."

That certainly peaked Shar's interest, which showed through the gleaming smile on her face.

"Really?"

"Yes honey. I gave a little eye contact and a smile on my way back as they were watching me."

"Manny, you are mess."

"I may not be looking for love and the happily ever after, but a good-looking companion won't hurt."

"Yeah, I hear you. Well, I don't know about you but I'm feeling full. I told Asher to get us some boxes."

"I know, this is a lot of food. It looks like dinner is taken care of tonight."

"Okay!"

"I wanted a piece of that German Chocolate cake though."

"You can get it to go."

"I sure can, but I don't know if they have a box big enough."

With a look of confusion on her face, Shar said, "Why wouldn't they have a box for a slice of cake?"

Shar threw her napkin across the table at Maniya and said, "Girl please, you need to stop. I thought you were talking about a real slice of cake. What am I going to do with you?"

They laughed, finished their drinks, and waited for Asher to return to their table.

Galvi and Ezekiel paid for their meals and made their way towards the exit. They came around the bar and up the middle aisle to pass the tables near the waterfall.

"It's crazy G, I swear that girl looks like the one you were dancing with last night."

"It's possible, but I honestly don't remember what she looked like. I mean, I know she was cute with a hellavah shape, but that's all I got."

Ezekiel reached for his phone but it wasn't on the clip. Stopping in his tracks, Ezekiel said, "Hey Galvi do you have my phone? Maybe I can look Shar up and find some pics before we go."

"Nah man, I don't have it. What are the chances that fate would bring the two of you face to face again anyway?"

"What about it and better yet, where's my phone?"

Galvi laughed a little and suggested that Ezekiel go check the bar. Ezekiel went back to the bar and his phone was exactly where he left it.

"Thank God," he said. Ezekiel tried to get Galvi's attention by waving his phone in the air like a kid on Christmas day, but Galvi was deep into a message on his phone. He might've missed Galvi's attention, but he did manage to grab the attention of a young lady in a flowing turquoise dress standing by a table.

"Why is this man waving at me from across the room?"

"Where," asked Maniya as she turned around to catch a glimpse?

"You can't miss him."

"Um that's one of the chocolate drops I was telling you about, the other one is the cake I wanted."

Ezekiel stopped waving and began walking back toward Galvi.

"Shut up Manny."

"Hey, I got it. It was still on the bar," said Ezekiel when he reached Galvi.

"Cool, let me finish sending this message."

"Shar I think they are coming this way, how do I look?"

Shar looked at Maniya and said, "Ravishing darling, but I'm leaving this to you because I need to go to the ladies room before we go."

"No Shar, you can't leave me here. What am I going to say?"

"Oh Manny, I'm sure you'll think of something."

Shar walked off in their direction with every intention to go to the restroom, but as she got closer to crossing the path of the gentlemen, she noticed something familiar about them. She had a sudden flashback of being on the dance floor last night. In that instant, it came to her and fate would have it that Shar and Ezekiel were looking into each other's eyes, once again.

"Shar," Ezekiel said astonishingly.

"Ezekiel, oh my goodness," replied Shar with a look of surprise. Galvi was in disbelief, thinking to himself, "Wow, chance really came through for him."

"You look great. I was literally just talking to my brother about you."

"Is that so?"

"Yes it is. Somehow, I knew chance would put us face to face again. You remember my brother Galvi?"

Shar looked at Galvi, "Yes, I do. How are you?"

"I'm well and you?"

"Wonderful, thanks for asking."

Maniya was a little concerned that the gentlemen hadn't passed the table yet, and curiosity got the best of her. She turned around and saw Shar smiling and talking to the chocolate drops, as if she knew them or something.

"Uhh, what in the hell is that about? I knew she should have stayed here a minute longer," she said.

"Listen, it's great seeing you but I was on my way to the restroom," said Shar trying to be calm and polite, hoping that he couldn't see or hear her heart pounding.

"Trust me, the pleasure is all mine and I don't want to hold you up. But I can't leave here today without giving you my number. He took out a business card and wrote his cell phone number on the back and handed it to Shar. "Call me. I really would like to get to know you."

Shar gladly accepted the card, smiled and said, "I most certainly will."

Shar walked away to the lady's room with a smile that could have landed her a role on the best toothpaste commercial. From the looks of it, Ezekiel could've joined her.

"Man, E, you called it, didn't you?"

Sticking his chest out boldly and widening his smile was his choice to show an affirming reply, as he watched Shar walk away.

"Hey, let's see what's on this side before we leave," said Galvi, as he directed Ezekiel to the opposite side of Shar and Maniya's table.

"Cool."

The men ventured to the other side and left the restaurant through a side exit. They were unwaveringly convinced that the exceptional experience and ambiance confirmed that the expansion of DESTINY would be an investment opportunity they couldn't afford to miss.

Meanwhile, Maniya was still at the table waiting for Shar to return, the gentleman to pass by or something. She didn't want to look back, but she couldn't help it. To her dismay, when she turned around, Shar and the chocolate drops were gone. "Where did they go?" she asked.

"I'm not sure, but I'm here," replied Asher.

Maniya turned around and Asher was standing at the table with the checks for the meals, two containers, and two bags.

"Is everything okay?" he asked.

"Yes, everything is fine. We had a great time. The service, food, and atmosphere were priceless."

"Thank you, that means a lot. Is there anything else I can do for you?'

"You've taken care of everything."

Before Shar exited the lady's room, she glanced at the business card and read, "Ezekiel R. Anderson, Family Business Investment Firm, Founder. When she flipped the card over she saw his number and a message that read he would be waiting.

"Awwwww," she said and did a little shuffle with an elaborate smile on her face. Then, she got herself together, cleared her throat, finger-combed her hair behind her ear, and walked out with composure.

"I wonder if Manny said something when they passed by," she thought. "I can't believe she didn't recognize who they were when she saw them at the bar," she continued.

As she made her way back to the table, she tried not to appear too anxious to share her encounter and find out if Maniya talked to them or not. When she got to the table, she noticed that the checks were there and Maniya was still in her seat, but her demeanor was different.

"Manny, what's wrong? What happened?"

"Do you really have to ask? What did you say to those guys? They never came this way."

"Is that it? Well, cheer up, because you are not going to believe this."

"This better be good."

"Trust me it is. What if I told you that you've already met those chocolate drops?"

Maniya looked at Shar with curiosity, "What do you mean? You mean… nah, it can't be. Can it?"

Shar was trying her best to hold it in. "What? Tell me what you're thinking."

"Those were the guys from last night."

"Oh my God yes!" said Shar with excitement, with hands trembling and everything.

"Get out."

"I'm not kidding, that was Ezekiel and his brother Galvi, the one you danced with."

"I clearly had more to drink than I thought because, from what I saw today, I would have passed on the cheesecake and devoured the German Chocolate instead."

"Manny please, I know you don't do one-night stands, do you?"

"Girl, no, but that might have been the first time. Hell, I might try anything with him.

"Damn, this is so crazy; you seemed to care less about any connection with him last night."

"That is kinda crazy huh? Maybe it's the, nah I'll just blame it on the alcohol." They laughed and smiled at the thought. Then, Shar said, "But, wait a minute, I didn't get to the best part."

She pulled out the business card and said playfully, "I got the digits this time. Oohh he wants to get to know me better and he's the founder of an investment firm."

"What?"

"Yes ma'am, not only is he tall and gorgeous, but he's educated, business minded, and a gentleman."

"Honey, that sounds like a winner Shar. This is exciting."

"I know right?"

"I can only hope that his brother is a reflection of the rest of his traits, because I know he's tall and gorgeous."

"Yes and his name is Galvi."

"Galvi, well that's different. I like that; it sounds like there is a meaning behind it."

"Yeah, it's cool. Anyway we should be leaving. Is the driver out there?"

"He should be, I mean we did leave our bags in the car."

"Oh yeah, okay, let's pay for the food and then we can go."

"Already done honey."

Shar looked surprised at the gesture, "Awww thank you Manny, you're too much."

"Don't mention it, that's what best friends are for." They grabbed their purses and doggy-bags and exited the lavish establishment with pleasure written on their faces. When they stepped outside, Zhamin was waiting. The timing could not have been more perfect.

Chapter 9

6:00 pm

"Wow, what a day," Maniya said as she plopped down on the sofa with her bags in her hand.

"You ain't kidding. We have been on the go, but it's been fun."

"Yeah, I'm glad you're enjoying your stay."

"It has been amazing. But I must say, if we are going out tonight, I am going to need to rest a little."

"You and me both. Hold on a minute, you're not going to call…"

"Shhh," said Shar before Maniya could finish what she was saying.

"What do you mean 'shhh'? All that excitement you showed at DESTINY, really chic?"

"I'm going to get to it, in due time. There's no need to rush, right?"

"In due time my behind. We have been hearing that since we were young, from everybody especially Aunt B. 'You'll have more than you can handle up there, in due time,'" she mocked," 'there'll be plenty of time to date, in due time.' 'You'll get a car, in due time,'" added Shar. "'The man of your dreams is coming, in due time,'" they said synchronously, followed by smiles and laughter.

"Shar, if you ask me my dear, that due time might very well be the present."

"I know, I know. I guess I'm just a little nervous and don't want to be too forward."

"Honey, he has already shown you that he's interested. Besides, you gotta arrange something for all of us to connect, okay?"

"Ah-ha, I knew there was a catch. You can experience love like I know both of us deserve."

"Here you go with that mushy stuff."

"Come on Manny, what about the double wedding we always talked about having when we were dreamy little girls, huh?"

"Lord help her," Maniya said as she got off the sofa. "I'm going to take a nap."

"Really?"

"Yes, really. See you soon and be ready to talk about something else."

Shar picked up a pillow from the sofa and threw it at Maniya.

"Hey, watch it," said Maniya.

They both laughed and went in their rooms to rest up before later.

Chapter 10

7:00pm

Galvi and Ezekiel were at the BGC when Ezekiel's phone rang.

"Hello?"

"Hello darling, how are you?"

"Hey ma," he said with a big smile on his face. "I'm fine, how are you? Are you enjoying your trip?"

"Oh baby, I'm fine and I'm having a wonderful time in Europe. I wish you and your brother were here with me."

"I know ma, we had some business deals to handle and our trips to the BGC are really crucial right now."

"I know. I shouldn't be selfish. I'm truly proud of you boys. I just know your father is smiling down on both of you."

"Hey ma, Galvi's here. Do you want to talk to him?" Ezekiel asked, trying not to tear up.

"Of course, I can always count on you two being close by."

"Hold on."

Galvi takes the phone, "Hey ma, how's my special lady?"

"She's fine, but she would be doing better if you told her you've found someone special to call your own."

"Ma, come on now, you know my focus is on business right now."

"Well, that doesn't stop me from praying for you and your brother. You know, mama's getting up in age. I'm not going to always be there to cook your favorite meals and encourage you to face your fears."

"Oh, here you go talking crazy."

"I'm not talking crazy son, it's the God's honest truth. You need a mate, and so does your brother. I want to enjoy some grandkids while I still can."

Silence took over the call and Galvi was deep in thought.

"Hello, baby, are you there? Can you hear me?"

"Yes, mama, I'm here. How are you enjoying the trip?"

"The trip is wonderful. I was just telling your brother that I wish the two of you were here."

"Yeah, that would've been nice ma. Maybe we can make it happen next time."

"Yeah, maybe next time with an extended family. The both of you can come with your wives and your children."

"Ma!"

"Ummmhuh, I didn't forget what we were talking about, and you better not either. Put me on speaker."

"Ezekiel, mom wants me to put the phone on speaker," he called out.

Ezekiel made his way over to Galvi and they stepped outside to finish the call.

"Ma, you're on speaker," said Ezekiel.

"Mama just wanted to let both of you know that I love you both so much. I can't wait to give you big hugs when I get home. Keep doing your very best, and I'm still praying for you. Talk to you soon."

"Thank you mama, we love you too. See you soon," they said and ended the call.

"Man, mama is still tripping on me about settling down."

"She's not tripping G. She's just loving you. She just wants the best for us, you know that."

"I know, but I hate to hear her talk about not being with us much longer and all of that, because I don't like it."

"Yeah, you have a point there. I don't like it either but, like it or not, it is reality."

"Look E, I need you to help with the situation. Ya feel me?"

Ezekiel put his arm around his brother and said, "Come on man, everything will work out." They walked back inside the BGC.

The kids and volunteers were all gathered in the conference room and awaited their return. Ezekiel and Galvi stepped in with smiles that raised the roof, and small conversations that filled the air ceased.

"My brother and I would like to thank each and every one of you for your commitment and believing that your possibilities are endless," said Ezekiel.

"We are living proof," Galvi chimed in.

"We want you to keep your dreams alive and goals in front of you. When you do that, great things will happen.

"With that being said," Galvi added, "we would like to present the Triple I&M, 'I Invested In Me' Award to the following seniors: Reginald Baldwin, Kesha Smith, Shawn Jackson, Dev Myers and Tia Perez."

The recipients stood up and joined Galvi and Ezekiel at the front of the room when their names were called. Galvi and Ezekiel shook their hands and presented them with personalized plaques that acknowledged their achievements.

"Congratulations and thank you for believing in yourselves as much as we do. You all have a full ride at UPENN as well as $1,000 added to your savings account."

The recipients smiled and shed tears of happiness while the younger members were looked at them with amazement in their eyes. Everyone cheered and applauded the occasion. Galvi and Ezekiel could not feel any better.

"Brother, what a blessing it is to be able to give back," said Ezekiel.

"I know, it's truly a blessing."

The crowd began to settle down and Galvi seized the opportunity to say some closing remarks.

"Thank you so much for welcoming us today. As always, remember to keep investing in yourself, and the payoff is priceless. See you soon."

Galvi and Ezekiel hi-fived a few students before leaving out.

"Man." said Galvi, "It's a great feeling to have when you are making a positive difference in someone's life."

"It sure is, G."

"What are you about to do now?"

"Not sure, I am thinking about hitting the gym for a late workout."

"Sounds good. Are we going to go out later?"

"Possibly, but I'm hoping to hear from Shar, I did give her my number."

"Yeah you did. Well, be patient and she might call you."

"I don't want to appear desperate, but I really would like to see her if I can."

"I gotcha, just let me know. I'm going to head home."

"Cool, I will. Be safe."

"Yo."

They both got in their cars and drove off in opposite directions.

Ezekiel set his radio to contemporary jazz to soothe him, while he crept through the evening traffic. He couldn't stop smiling as he tapped to the melody on his steering wheel with thoughts of Shar smiling and laughing in his presence. "It sure would be nice to hear from her," he thought. As he gazed out the window, the streetlights appeared to be dancing with the dark skies, which set the perfect stage for romance.

Chapter 11

9:05 pm

"It is so beautiful here," Shar said as her eyes followed the ripples of the waves.

"Only the best for my baby. The ocean is endless like my love for you," he said in a raspy deep soothing voice. He wrapped his arms around her waist and leaned down to kiss her on her right earlobe. Shar closed her eyes, leaned back into his chest, and allowed herself to become the air he breathed.

She could've fallen asleep in his arms at that moment with the sand between her toes and the sound of the waves caressing against the shore.

"Baby," Shar said as she turned around and rested her arms on his shoulders, "I'm glad you are here with me."

"There's no other place I'd rather be than right here with you," he said as he lifted her up and planted a kiss on her lips so wet and juicy, the ocean was jealous.

"What in the world?" Maniya saw Shar gripping her pillow tightly and kissing it like it was Denzel.

"Shar, Shar," she said as she nudged at Shar's shoulder to try to wake her up. "Shar," she said for the last time.

"Huh, hello, what is it?" Shar replied as she rubbed her eyes trying to figure out what happened to the beach. She sat up and looked Maniya in the eyes with a look of disappointment. She grabbed her pillow to cover her face and fell back on the mattress screaming, "Why, why, why, Manny?! Why do I keep having these dreams that feel so real? For once, I want to wake up and see him lying next to me or bringing me a tray of bacon, eggs, toast and orange juice wearing nothing but a smile."

"It can, and it will, happen for you if that's what you want. Look at it this way, you could be having nightmares instead."

Shar removed the pillow from her face and smiled.

"Now, while you were in here dreaming your life away, I've been trying to think of something for us to do tonight. You only have a few more days here and you're supposed to enjoy every moment. Because, Lord knows the boredom awaiting you back home."

"Shut up Manny," Shar said jokingly. "What time is it anyway?"

"It's a little after 9."

"Are you serious? I took a longer nap than I thought."

"Yep. So no more time to waste, what do you want to do?"

"Hmmm, I don't know. I wish I could be back on that beach with my chocolate dream."

"Well, I don't know about the beach part. But you do have the number of a certain someone who is interested. Maybe…"

"Maybe what Manny?"

"I'm just saying, maybe you can call him and the two of you can get to know each other better or something?"

Shar sighed deeply and closed her eyes and thought of the possibilities. "I don't know Manny. Do you think I should call him?"

"Shar, by now I would think that you know I'm for you going after what you want. So, I shouldn't have a say anymore."

Shar took Ezekiel's business card from her purse and stared at it for a moment.

Maniya headed for the door and said, "I'm going to let you figure it out. Just let me know what you want to do, I'll be waiting up front. I think I'm going to heat up some of my leftovers."

"Okay, that sounds good. Give me a moment."

Shar didn't waste too much time before she started to dial Ezekiel's number. The phone rang four times without an answer and just as she was about to hang up, she heard a voice say, "Hello?"

"Hello," she said in return. A little awkward silence passed then she continued, "Ezekiel?"

"Yes this is he."

"Hi, this is Shar."

If she could have seen his smile through the phone, her dim lit room would have illuminated.

"Hey Shar, how are you?"

"I'm well, and you?"

"I'm great, especially now that I'm hearing your voice."

"Awww, that's sweet of you."

"It's true. I must say, seeing you today was such a gift. I was hoping that I would hear from you soon."

"It was good seeing you too. DESTINY is a really nice place. We enjoyed it."

"Were you there with your friend that was at Club Breezy?"

"Yeah I was with her. She's been trying to make sure I have a great time while I'm here."

"That is so crazy."

"What?"

"No, my brother was intrigued by her in the restaurant. I told him that she looked familiar."

Shar started laughing. "Yeah, that is crazy because Manny felt the same way."

"Did they really drink that much or what?"

"I have no idea. But at least now they can say that attraction goes beyond the alcohol."

"That's true, and the same goes for me and you."

"I can't disagree there," said Shar blushingly.

"Hey, I have an idea. Let's all go listen to some jazz and get to know one another better."

"That sounds exciting."

"Great, let me call my brother."

"Okay and I'll tell Manny."

"Sounds great, I'll call you in about 15 minutes to confirm a time and get the address where I can send my driver to pick you ladies up."

"Wonderful, I'll talk to you then."

Shar ended the call and ran up front to tell Manny the news.

"Manny! Oh my God in heaven, I called him and he wants us to go out with him and his brother to listen to some jazz in the city."

"Yeah?"

"Yes, and he's going to send a car for us."

"A car?"

"Yes, and he says that his brother noticed you at DESTINY too."

"Hot damn, now we're talking."

"He's going to call me back in a few moments to give me the details and he needs the address to give to the driver.

They grabbed each other's hands and jumped up and down, smiling from ear to ear as if they were back in grade school.

"Okay, let's get our composure back," said Shar.

"You're right," said Maniya after clearing her throat.

"We need to find something fierce to wear chic."

"I was thinking about that jumpsuit I bought today."

"Okay, let's see."

Shar grabbed her bags from her room and joined Maniya to put together her outfit for the evening.

"Bammm," said Shar, "I got my coral jumpsuit with my pearl T-strapped heels."

"Don't forget your accessories."

"Awww, I didn't bring my pearl drop earrings."

"No worries, I got you." Maniya said while going through her jewelry box to grab pearl earrings.

"Perfect," said Shar. "Now what have you decided on?"

"I'm going to jazz it up, too. I choose this black-out number."

"This one," said Shar, pointing at the ensemble hanging on Maniya's closet door.

"Yes indeed, simple yet jazzy. Ya know, black sleek fitted cigarettes and the black sateen wrap top. Cute, right?"

"Yes, it is, I love black on black. What shoes?"

Maniya reached into her closet, hit a switch, and revealed this hidden area of shoes. "Now, that's the real question."

"Manny, when did you get all of these shoes, my lord. I thought I was bad, but I think you have me beat."

Maniya laughed and said, "I honestly couldn't begin to tell you. One day I just remember needing to call a company to add some space for them. Anyway, enough of that, just come help me pick out a pair."

"Well, if you want to a little color, you can go with these," pointing at a pair of color-blocked heels. "Nah, I think I want something sparkly."

"OK, how about these?" pointing at a pair of heels with reflecting rhinestones, "what do you think?"

"Yesszz, now we're talking."

"What's that noise?" asked Maniya.

"What noise?"

"You don't hear it, it's like a ding, ding, da ding ding, da ding ding."

"Oh that's my phone ringing. I forgot I changed the ring tone."

"You better hurry up and catch it. It might be your chocolate dream."

Shar ran to the other room and answered the phone. "Hello?"

"Hey Shar, it's E, Ezekiel."

"Hey there."

"I hope I didn't take too long to get back to you, but everything is good on my end with Galvi and all. Did you talk to your friend? What's her name again?"

"Maniya."

"That's right, have you talked to Maniya yet?"

"Yes, she's in."

"This should be great."

"I know, I'm counting on it."

"I can have the car to you ladies in about an hour. You're in Manhattan, right?"

"Oh yeah, yes we are. You need the address, don't you? Give me a minute."

"Manny," Shar called out, "Come here, I need the address."

Maniya came into the room and gave Shar a piece of mail with the address on it. "OK, I have it. The address is 1214 5th Ave, WMI Estates."

"Perfect, I know where that is. If you'd prefer, the driver can get there sooner."

"No, an hour is great. We'll be downstairs around 10."

"He'll be there waiting. Can't wait to see you."

"Likewise."

"Oh yeah, I almost forgot. Just so you know, we'll be at Jazz@Lincoln Center. There are a few nice spots there."

"Great, see you in a little while."

They ended the call and continued to prepare for an enriching evening.

"OK Manny, we have an hour to get ready."

"I'm on it."

"Can you bump my hair please?"

"Sure thing."

The ladies got ready with little time to spare. They checked themselves out in the mirror and blew kisses at their reflections before grabbing their clutches and heading downstairs.

"I must say, we look marvelous darling."

"Truly. We surely have come a long way from stuffing bras with tissue."

"Tell me about it."

"Aunt B was right. There was no need to rush certain parts to develop, we would fill out."

"In due time," they said in harmony.

"Do you remember that?" Shar asked with a little laughter.

"Yes. Wow, it seems like it was just yesterday."

"Well, she didn't lie about that. But it was so hard to be patient then."

"That's so true. Now, we have more than we can handle, hips and ass too."

"Speak for yourself honey, I love all of mine and I handle it just fine," she said as she outlined her body with her hands.

Maniya laughed and said, "You know what I mean Shar. You don't get tired of men coming on to you because of how you look?"

"Let me think about it. Nah, it's flattering as long as they don't cross the line or assume that because I look good, I'm not intelligent."

"Ooh, I hate that."

"Enough of that nonsense, let's go have a good time with some fine, intelligent brothers."

"Let's go."

"Manny, you are a trip. All of that talk about getting tired of men coming on to you because of how you look and you were ready to eat a slice of German Chocolate Cake, a.k.a. Galvi, without utensils or your hands.

"Hush," Maniya said, "I know, I know. I'm gonna do better!"

The ladies laughed gently as they exited the building.

Chapter 12

10:15 pm

"What better way to complement the evening than with two beautiful ladies," a voice called out.

To their surprise, Ezekiel and Galvi were leaning against a stretched Range Rover, holding a red rose for each of them. The brothers stepped forward as the ladies approached them, kissed them on the cheek, and handed them their roses.

The ladies looked stunning and Ezekiel and Galvi didn't waste any time to tell them. Shar and Maniya were in for a night to remember, because these fine gentlemen were looking good and smelling better. They were both tempted to just invite them up for a night cap, but they didn't.

"Galvi, it's a pleasure to meet you again. I'm Maniya."

"The pleasure is all mine Maniya."

"Thank you for the rose, that was very sweet."

"You're welcome. I firmly believe that a lady should be treated like a queen. Shall we?" asked Galvi as he led Maniya to an open car door.

Ezekiel grabbed Shar's hand gently. "Thank you for the rose," said Shar as she was trying to stop the electrifying impulses she was feeling as his hand touched hers.

"You are more than welcome. I wanted to give you something that compliments your beauty inside and out."

"It's beautiful," she said as she admired the big bloomed velvet red rose.

"Well, let's go listen to some great jazz. Are you a jazz fan?" asked Ezekiel as he escorted Shar to the car.

"I love jazz. It has helped me wine down and feel joyous many times over."

"Are you in the mood for dancing?"

"Hmmm, that's something you are going to have to find out for yourself,' said Shar as she entered the car. Ezekiel followed her and everyone was inside and ready to go.

"Lincoln Center it is," Ezekiel said to the driver. They all enjoyed the ride with conversation, smiles, and laughter. After a scenic route through the city, the driver had them at the Lincoln Center just before 11 o'clock.

The gentlemen took the ladies by their hands and proudly escorted them into Dizzy's. The evening was off to a great start. The cool crisp air paired with the night lights dancing through the moonlit sky, everything set the perfect stage.

The sounds that seeped out of Dizzy's music box was just a hint of the full experience that was captured inside. The lighting was soft, the aroma was enticing, and the music was golden. Ezekiel reserved a table that overlooked Central Park, which contained an immaculate view.

Shar and Maniya felt like the queens they were while in the presence of Ezekiel and Galvi. They made sure to show the ladies that chivalry was very much alive, by pulling out their chairs and catering to their requests before their own.

"This view is great."

"It certainly is," said Maniya.

"Do you guys come here often?" asked Shar.

"As much as I can," said Ezekiel.

"Same here," said Galvi, "And, unfortunately, it's not often enough for either of us."

"But we do enjoy it when we can come."

"Is this the first time you've been here Maniya?" Galvi asked.

"Actually, it is, but it won't be the last," she said as she tapped her fingers on the table to the beat the quartet was delivering.

"Man, instead of being homesick, I'm going to be New York sick when I go home," said Shar with a little pout.

"This is your first time here too, I take it."

"Yes, and we have nothing like this in Eatonville."

"I think I've heard of that, where is it exactly?" Ezekiel asked.

"It's a small town in Florida."

"Yeah, it was the first black town established after Emancipation right?" asked Galvi.

"Yeah, that's right. I knew it sounded familiar."

"Home sweet home. It's historical, which is great but there's not much to do there."

"Don't remind me Manny."

"Oh, Maniya are you from there too?"

"Yep, that's how we met, almost 23 years ago."

"Wow, it's crazy how time flies. It seems like we were just passing each other on our bikes with the matching pink and white streamers coming from the handle bars."

"Okayyy," said Maniya with a little laughter. "And you can't forget the baskets in front."

"Oh my gosh, the baskets," Shar said before closing her eyes briefly and smiling, as if it was her cue that she had the memory on replay.

"Man you ladies have been friends for a long time." They nodded in agreement as their waitress approached the table to service them.

"Good evening ladies and gentlemen. Welcome to Dizzy's. I hope that you are enjoying yourselves so far."

"Yes we are, thank you," they said collectively.

"May I interest the ladies with a complimentary glass of Riesling?" The ladies nodded yes and as the waitress proceeded to pour the wine, she asked the gentlemen what they were having.

"I'll have a crown and coke," said Ezekiel and Galvi chimed in to say make it two. She topped off the wine glasses and told the gentlemen that she would have their drinks right out for them.

"Please take a look at the appetizer menus and I'll be back with you shortly."

"Sounds great, thank you," said Ezekiel pausing briefly as he looked for a nametag. "I'm sorry, what was your name again?"

"Oh no, my apologies, I think it slipped my mind and I didn't say it earlier. My name is Faith."

Shar and Maniya glanced at each other at the same time and Ezekiel finished his statement.

"Thank you Faith."

"You're welcome, I'll have those drinks right out for you."

Ezekiel looked to his left and saw Shar gazing out of the window at Central Park. Her twinkling eyes switched focus back to Dizzy's interior as the saxophonist began to play. Ezekiel enjoyed the simple beauty in her smile and elegance as she surveyed the room and swayed her upper body to the melodious sound.

"Are you having a good time?"he asked her as he reached out to touch her hand. Shar smiled and said, "I'm enjoying every minute of it."

Galvi and Maniya were smiling and laughing together and rocking to the music. "I think it's great that the two of you have such a strong friendship," said Galvi.

"It is awesome, we're like sisters. True friendship is hard to come by, but it's evident when it has survived the highs and lows in each person's life, you know?"

"I do. The two of you remind me of my brother and I. We have been together through it all. Do you have any siblings?"

"No, we're both the only child in our families."

"Cool"

"Yeah, I think that's one of the reasons we share such a great bond."

The waitress came back to the table with drinks and a big smile on her face.

"Here you are, sorry for the delay. I have a crown and coke for you and you," she said as she placed the drinks in front of the gentlemen.

"Has everyone decided on any appetizers?"

"I'm not that hungry, are you Shar?" asked Ezekiel.

"Not really but we can get something for the table at least.

"Galvi, Maniya, do the two of you want anything in particular?"

"Nah, it doesn't matter," replied Galvi as Maniya nodded her head no.

"OK well we'll have some honey roasted mixed nuts, salted peanuts and the N'awlins Fry."

"Excellent choices. Can I get any of you anything else?"

They all said no and placed the menus to the side.

"Great, I'll have your order out for you momentarily."

The sextet was in the groove of things on stage and from the looks of it everyone in the audience, even the workers, was enjoying every moment of it. The music began to get softer and the orchestrator's voice came through the mic.

"How's everyone feeling? Is everyone feeling alright?"

The crowd responded in unison, "Yeah."

"I'm glad to hear that and I hope all of you are ready for a great night of entertainment." The crowd responded with words, whistles and hand claps.

"Thank you for being here tonight ladies and gents. It is always our pleasure to have you; we hope you are enjoying yourselves in the company of great jazz musicians who are gracing you with their presence and talents this evening. Well I don't know about you but this is my favorite part of the session. I hope you haven't gotten too comfortable in your seats because it's time to get up and really let the music move you."

The musicians began to increase the beat and the volume and people started to get out of their seats and let the music seduce them.

"This should be fun," said Ezekiel. He took Shar's hand and they joined the fun. Maniya and Galvi were right behind them. The mixture of the drums, sax, piano, bass and scatting was a musical foreplay at its best. Ezekiel got the answer to his question about Shar's mood for dancing when she took the floor and let loose. Her hips were swaying sensually and cohesively with her upper body with every step she took.

Ezekiel wanted to grab her close to feel her body next to his but he didn't want to come on too strong, so he allowed her a little space. She turned away from him as if she was dancing away but she didn't go too far before finding her way back to his parameters.

Shar came closer and put her arms around Ezekiel's neck as if she could read his mind. He put his arms around her waist and embraced their physical connection. They let the music move them into dimensions that neither of them had experienced in quite some time. It was clear to anyone bearing witness that they were truly enjoying the moment and each other.

"They look really good together, don't they?" asked Maniya as she danced hand to hand resting her head on Galvi's chest.

"They do and as a matter of fact, we don't look too bad ourselves," he said with a smile. He extended his arms, sending Maniya out just enough to admire her from a short distance. Galvi turned her around and brought her back toward him with his arms wrapped around her. Maniya leaned the back of head on his chest and rocked with him side to side, to the sexy rhythm. Feeling caught in the moment, Maniya closed her eyes and thought, "Is this what love really feels like?"

Faith was bringing the food to the table as the number was coming to a close. Ezekiel and Shar greeted Faith and ordered all of them another round of drinks. Ezekiel picked up a shrimp off the plate and paused. "Do you like seafood?"

"I love it." He proceeded to bring the shrimp closer to her mouth so that she could take a bite. Shar opened her mouth and took a bite. She closed her eyes as she chewed the shrimp, taking in the Cajun flavors. "Mmmmm, thank you, it's really good."

Ezekiel smiled and took a sip of his drink. He was hoping that she didn't notice how he was staring at her lips as she chewed the shrimp. They were looking so appetizing; he wanted to bite into them. Shar picked up an oyster and returned the favor of being fed to Ezekiel.

Galvi and Maniya came back to the table a little flushed. They grabbed a few peanuts and took a sip of their drinks. "Woooo, these guys are going in tonight, one great set after another," said Galvi.

"Yeah it's great, I couldn't imagine enjoying it in better company," said Ezekiel as he touched Shar's hand.

"You said it," added Galvi, as he placed his hand on Maniya's.

"Are you ladies having a good time?"

"A marvelous time."

"Truly," added Shar.

"I know. The two of you are giving us a run for our money on the dance floor," said Ezekiel.

"That's right, enjoying every minute of it," said Shar.

They all laughed and started tapping and rocking to the music. "Wow, where does the time go? It's almost 2 o'clock," said the host for the evening, and you know what that means."

"Yeah," the crowd shouted. "It's time for the Late Night Session to turn it up a notch. How you feelin?"

"Great," the crowd yelled.

Each player on set played a mini-solo starting with the saxophone and ending with the drums. The vocalist started to scat and all the musicians fell into place, creating a chemistry that exuded across the entire room. The audience displayed a charismatic energy through the smiles on their faces, the connection of hands, bobbing of heads and tapping of their feet. There was full engagement and intense intimacy unspoken. Shar could feel the temperature rising' but she wasn't the only one. "Wooh, is it getting hot in here or is it just me?" she asked.

"I don't think so," said Maniya. "I was thinking the same thing."

Galvi took a napkin and wiped his forehead and Ezekiel adjusted himself in his seat. They all reached for their glasses to finish their drinks in a temporary moment of awkwardness. As the music started to simmer the host got on the mic.

"Ladies and gentlemen, it has been my extreme pleasure to host the Late Night Session here at Dizzy's for you this evening. I truly hope that you enjoyed yourselves and you let the music carry you to a place of extreme satisfaction. Until the next time we meet, good night."

A round of applause echoed throughout the room accompanied with a standing ovation. The sextet on stage took a bow and extended their arms to shake hands of the people who approached them. The lights came on and people started to clear out of Dizzy's; Shar, Ezekiel, Galvi and Maniya included.

They felt a nice cool breeze under the starry skies when they stepped outside. The disbursed crowd was still smiling as they walked and talked about how much they enjoyed themselves. Some of the people strolled around Central Park while others departed in their vehicles. Shar, Maniya and their dates were a part of the latter.

Ezekiel and Galvi were true gentlemen. They opened the doors for the ladies and made sure they were safe before leaving. Once everyone was inside the vehicle, Ezekiel signaled the driver to go. The driver already knew to take the scenic route back to the ladies' residence, so he coasted along the city, circling Central Park and capturing the essence of the cityscape throughout the blocks. The ladies and gentlemen were relaxed in their seats, taking in the moment. Ezekiel opened the moon-roof to expose the starry night during the drive.

"This is really beautiful," said Shar.

"It truly is," Maniya added.

"Let me know if it gets to chilly and I'll close it." Galvi caught himself gazing at Maniya and feeling something moving that shouldn't be, well it should be but not right now.

He shifted his position in his seat and Maniya moved a little closer to him. If his brother and Shar were not in the car there's no telling what he and Maniya would be doing, but he had a few strong ideas. "Hey bro, you alright over there? You're mighty quiet."

"Yeah man, I'm good just taking it all in." He grabbed Maniya's hand and said, "I hope you enjoyed yourself tonight, I know I did."

"Well the feeling is mutual. I enjoyed or should I say, I'm enjoying myself very much," said Maniya as she rested her head on his shoulder.

"What is she trying to do to me," he thought. "Whatever it is, I think it is working. He gently ran his fingertips down her arm until their fingertips met.

"Lord help me. My body is telling me to mount this man's shoulders and give him some mouth-watering dessert while I get a closer look at the stars," Maniya thought to herself as she crossed her legs and bit her bottom lip.

"Shar are you OK? Are you comfortable?" asked Ezekiel.

"Yes, I'm fine."

Little did he know her mind had escaped back to her beach dream. She was in his arms and their tongues were crashing like waves and her body sank into his like feet in the sand. It's a good thing he called her name because there's no telling where her hands would've ended up.

"I've really enjoyed myself with you tonight. It's really refreshing to have a great evening with a beautiful woman and already be looking forward to the next time." Shar smiled but waited a moment before she said anything in response. "I mean I hope I'm not being to forward and that you feel the same way. I mean…" Shar place her pointer finger on Ezekiel's lips to quiet him. "Shhhh, I had a great time with you and I would love to see you again. I just wish I wasn't going back home in a couple of days. I'm having such a great time here."

Ezekiel returned the favor and placed his finger on her lips to quiet her. "We won't worry about what happens in a couple of days but we will focus on the here and now."

He leaned in to kiss her just as the driver stopped in front of Maniya's building.

"Wow that was quick, we're here already," said Maniya.

She wanted to invite Galvi up but she didn't want to appear too easy. She knew that if he came up at 3 o'clock in the morning that was going to lead to sex. Even though she wanted it so bad that she could feel and taste it, she needed to wait.

Galvi and Ezekiel helped the ladies out of the car and walked them up to the door of the building. "Thank you for a great evening."

"Yes, thank you, everything was wonderful. It feels good meeting great people for a change," said Maniya.

"Likewise," said Galvi as he gazed into Maniya's eyes.

"Hey do you guys want to come up for some coffee or tea?"

Maniya looked at Shar and thought to herself, "What in the hell is she thinking. If this man gets anywhere close to my room, hell my floor, I don't think I'm going to be able to control myself. Maybe they'll say no. Please say no, oooh Lord I'm trying to be good."

Shar noticed Maniya's look but it was too late, she couldn't take the offer back. Hell, she felt the same way. Shar couldn't believe she had suggested that, it's not even her place. There had to be something magical going on that evening because the guys responded at the same time. "Sure," they said in unison.

"Lord if this is a test, I might just fail. I'm just saying," Maniya thought. "Let me send the driver on, we'll call for service when we're ready. Ezekiel went to clear the driver to leave and came back to the door and they all went up to Maniya's place.

The ladies went in and told the gentlemen to make themselves comfortable before kicking off their heels and getting together the necessities to prepare the coffee and tea. "Girl, you know I'm going to kill you, right?" whispered Maniya. I know," she said quietly, but if you knew what I've been thinking, you might realize that I might beat you to it." They both laughed casually. "Are you getting those urges too?"

"Yes, Manny this is crazy and I've never had a one-night stand or anything like that."

"Well who says it has to be a one-nighter?"

They laughed again but this time they were a little louder than the last and they alarmed the guys. "Hey ladies are you all alright in there? Can we help with anything?"

"We're fine just need to know if you prefer coffee or tea."

"I'll have coffee, a nice bold one if you have it," said Galvi. "Any cream or sugar?"

"No cream but a few scoops of sugar will be fine."

"Got it, what about you Ezekiel?"

"I'll have the same."

"Okay, we'll have those out in a few. Shar what are you going to have?"

"I want some green tea with honey."

"I should have known. Put on the kettle for tea and I'll use the Keurig for the coffee."

"I love my Keurig; I didn't know you had one."

"Yeah, I decided to get one a few weeks ago after using the one at the office."

"Why don't you have it out?"

"I don't like to clutter my counter space and besides, I still like my old-fashion tea bags."

The kettle started whistling while Shar was putting the tea bags in the cups. She grabbed the honey from the cabinet, turned off the stove and picked up the kettle. She started to pour the honey and water into the cups at the same time; in her mind it made all the difference.

"Shar what are you doing?"

"Making tea."

Maniya laughed and said, "I know that but both hands?"

"Yeah, it makes the tea taste better."

"Ok girl, I'm done."

"You'll see."

The coffee was ready and the ladies carried them to Galvi and Ezekiel, who were sitting out on the balcony. Maniya turned on the forever-lit candles at the table after she gave Galvi his coffee.

"Thank you," Ezekiel said after Shar gave him his coffee.

"You're welcome, be careful it's hot."

He blew into the coffee cup before taking a sip.

"I'll be right back."

Galvi gave Maniya his thanks as well then she joined Shar in the kitchen.

"Shar, I'm trying to contain myself but it is so hard being around this gorgeous, intelligent, muscular, chocolate man and not want to pounce on him. He sends this tingling feeling throughout my body. Shar what is that?"

"Shhhh, I know. I know. I feel the same way and when Ezekiel looks at me it's like he's looking into my soul and that smile, Lord have mercy. I get that tingling feeling combined with pulsations and we…"

"Ummh Ok, hold the music. We got to get ourselves together."

They cleared their throats, shook themselves loose and grabbed some napkins and their tea.

"Ok let's go," said Shar.

"Right behind you, let me grab these Pirouettes to nibble on."

"Ooh are those the Pepperidge Farm Wafers we used to devour in college?"

"Yes ma'am."

"Great."

"Well there they are. We were beginning to think the two of you left us to drink coffee alone."

"We wouldn't do that," said Shar.

"We brought some napkins and Hazelnut Chocolate Wafers."

"Sounds great, let us help you with that," said Ezekiel.

He took the napkins from Maniya and everyone sat at the table and made themselves comfortable.

"This is a really nice view you have here Maniya,"

"Thanks Galvi."

"It's not as beautiful as you though," he added.

She smiled and changed the subject. "How's your coffee?"

"It's wonderful, thanks again."

"Same here," said Ezekiel.

They chatted, sipped on tea and coffee and nibbled on Hazelnut Chocolate Pirouettes for what seemed like a short moment. They were really comfortable with each other and conversation flowed as if they'd known one another for years. After the drinks were done, the two pairs moved to more intimate sections on the balcony to enjoy their company on a more personable level.

Shar laid against Ezekiel on a chaise at one end of the balcony while Maniya and Galvi lay facing each other on a wide recliner on the other end. Their conversations continued and before they knew it, the sun was rising.

"How about that, my first sunrise with you," said Ezekiel.

"It's beautiful."

Shar and Ezekiel looked over at Maniya and Galvi and they apparently made the same discovery because they were looking at the sunrise and smiling.

"Wow, this is the first," Maniya thought to herself. "I laid next to this fine man all night and enjoyed him with our clothes on, what's really going on?"

"I hope I didn't overstay my welcome," said Galvi.

"Of course not, why would you say such a thing? We had a beautiful time getting to know each other. I loved it."

"Me too, I hope it's not the last time."

"I'm sure it won't be," Maniya said as she got off the recliner to start clearing some things away.

"Shar, Ezekiel are you up over there?" Maniya called out to them.

"Yes we are." Shar replied as she got up to help. Ezekiel and Galvi were not far behind them with rising. They grabbed their cups and took them inside. Everyone exchanged how they enjoyed everything and agreed that they all should get some rest because if they didn't, they were going to feel it later. Ezekiel called for a car and he and Galvi kept the ladies company a little while longer while they waited. Shar and Maniya cleaned the dishes and tidied the kitchen smiling the entire time. The good energy they all felt was evident throughout Maniya's place. Everything felt right.

"Beep, beep, beep," sounded Ezekiel's phone. He took it out of his pocket and retrieved a message that stated the driver was downstairs. He signaled Galvi as he stood up and walked towards the kitchen to say goodbye.

"OK beautiful, the driver is here."

He leaned in to give Shar a hug and a kiss on the cheek. "I'll give you a call later."

"OK."

"Maniya," he said, "thanks for your hospitality."

"You're welcome."

Galvi was next to Maniya and he took her by the hand and kissed it gently. He thanked her for a lovely evening and gave her a hug.

"Get some rest and I'll call you a little later."

"OK sounds good."

The brothers left and Maniya and Shar slid down the nearest wall, wearing the biggest smiles on their faces.

"Oh my word," Maniya called out.

"Amen."

The ladies basked in the afterglow of simple 'good company' of great men who could enjoy the company of a woman without having sex. "I wonder if it was as hard for them as it was for us."

"I'm not sure but I know something else was hard."

They laughed and got off the floor.

"I'm done girl. I've got to lay down before I fall out."

"Me too, if I'm not up when you get up come check on me Shar."

"Will do; sweet dreams."

"Thanks, I can only imagine what kind of dreams you're going to have now," said Maniya casually throwing her hand up as she walked into her room.

Shar considered taking a shower before getting in the bed, but that didn't happen. Instead she slipped out of her clothes and threw on an oversized tee and lay down. She couldn't help but think about how yesterday unfolded and Ezekiel. "Could it be true?" she thought. "Have I finally met someone with a beautiful spirit, mind and body?" She wrapped her arms around her pillow tightly and closed her eyes.

Chapter 13

Sunday Afternoon

Ring, Ring, Ring.

"Hello I'm sorry I'm unable to take your call at this time, please leave a message and I'll return your call at my earliest convenience." Beep.

"Shar, hey baby, it's your mom. Shar baby call me as soon as you can. I love you."

It was just passed noon and Shar was sleeping hard.

Ring, Ring, Ring.

"Hello, I'm sorry I'm unable to take your call at this time, please leave a message and I'll return your call at my earliest convenience." Beep.

"Shar, baby it's mom again, please call me, it's about your father."

Now it was passed one o'clock and Shar was on the verge of getting up but not quite there yet and Maniya was still in a deep sleep.

Shar's phone rang again thirty minutes later, it was her mom again stressing the urgency for Shar to call her. Shar woke up to the sound of a message notification on her phone. She stretched her arms up and yawned before reaching for her phone. After she wiped her eyes, she sat up and looked at her phone screen.

Three missed calls from mom, what's going on?

Shar dialed her mom's number without listening to her messages, but there was no answer.

"Hey mom it's Shar, I'm trying to call you back. I was sleeping when you called. Call me back."

After she left the message, Shar checked her voice mail and listened to the messages her mom left. She sat on the end of the bed, trying not to panic, but gravely concerned about what was wrong with her father. She took a deep breath and tried to stay calm. She tried to call her mom back again, but her call was forwarded to voicemail. Shar was getting nervous. She hoped everything was okay but couldn't help but think about the worst possibilities.

"Why would mom call me like that if it wasn't anything serious?" she thought. Shar knows that her dad is diabetic but he controls it for the most part. He is also a cancer survivor of 5 years with no indication that it had resurfaced.

"I know they would've told me if the cancer came back, I just know they would've told me," cried Shar. She picked up her phone to attempt calling her mom again but changed her mind. She went to the bathroom to wash her face and brush her teeth. As she rinsed the soap from her face she said, "God, please let my parents be alright, please."

Ring, ring, ring.

Shar answered the phone anxiously without looking at the caller ID. "Hello, mom?"

"Shar, it's Ezekiel."

"Oh," she sighed as she plopped down on the bed. "Hey Ezekiel."

"Are you okay? You sound a little distraught. Is everything alright?"

"I wish I knew."

"What do you mean, you wish you knew?"

"I received several calls from my mom, well I missed the calls but the messages she left stressed that I needed to call her back immediately," explained Shar frantically.

"Did she say what it was concerning?"

"Well one of the messaged said that it was concerning my father. I've tried to call back several times since I woke up but she," said Shar starting to cry, "she's not picking up and I don't know what to think."

"Shar darling, breathe, try to stay calm. Where's Maniya?"

"She's still sleeping; I'm trying to keep it together. I thought that you were her when my phone rang," she said as she wiped the tears from her eyes.

"Do you want me to come over?"

"I don't know. I don't want to inconvenience you or put you out of your way."

"There's no inconvenience at all, don't think that way."

"I just need to get to the airport."

"Say no more, I'm on the way."

They ended the call and Shar took her phone into the bathroom while she took a quick shower. The phone did not ring. She tried to hold back the tears but she could not help but think of the worst possibilities.

"Why else would mom not answer?" she thought. "I just met someone that seems like he's everything I've wanted in a man and he lives here in New York and I have to go back to Florida and now even sooner than I planned," rambled the thoughts in her head. "God why is this happening now?"

She wiped her face, rinsed her body and turned off the shower. Just as she grabbed her towel, her phone rang.

Shar snatched her phone off the sink and answered it abruptly, still dripping wet.

"Hello, hello!"

"Shar baby, where have you been? I've been trying to call you."

"Mama what's going on? What's wrong with daddy? You've got me worried. I was sleeping when you called but I tried to reach you as soon as I saw the missed calls."

"I'm sorry to have to call you with this while you're on vacation baby, but."

"Ma, what is it?"

"Shar your father is in the hospital and it doesn't look too good."

"What do you mean? What do you mean?"

"It all happened so fast. I was out in the garden after breakfast for about an hour and when I came back in the house I found him unconscious on the living room floor."

"What?" "Oh my God," Shar murmured in disbelief as she dropped to the floor.

"I called 911 and when the paramedics arrived and checked his vitals, his glucose levels were through the roof. Baby he's in a coma."

"Oh my God, my God," she said getting louder with tears streaming down her face. Maniya heard the commotion and went immediately into Shar's room.

"Shar, what's wrong? Shar talk to me."

"Maniya," said Shar shaking her head. She couldn't manage to say anything else.

"What, what is it?" asked Maniya again.

"Shar, Shar," her mom called to her. "Can you get home? We're praying for the best but I don't know what God has planned baby."

"Mama please, do not say that. If something… if dad… I can't think about it. I'll be there as soon as I can. I'm about to go to the airport now."

"We're at Flagler Hospital right now, but he's being airlifted to Florida Hospital so get a flight to Orlando. Try to be strong baby, you know your father is a fighter."

"Yes ma'am," Shar said as she sniffled and wiped away the tears. Maniya extended her hand to help Shar off the floor trying to wait patiently for more information.

"I'll see you soon mama, kiss daddy for me and tell him I love him."

"I will baby."

"I love you."

"I love you too Shar."

They ended the call and Shar turned to Maniya and told her that her father was in a coma and things didn't look good. Maniya wrapped her arms around her friend and shed some tears discreetly.

"Shar honey, I'm sorry to hear that. It's going to be alright, have faith. You know I'm here for you."

"I'm trying. If anything happened to my dad, if he..."

"Shhhh, don't you dare, you know dad is not going anywhere. Don't even think that way."

"I have to get dressed and get out of here," said Shar as she broke away from the hug.

A series of abrupt knocks at the door startled the ladies.

"Who can that be? I'm not expecting anyone," said Maniya as she walked to the door.

Shar was putting on her clothes, trying to keep her face dry in the process. She wasn't thinking about who was at the door.

Then it came to her, "Oh Manny that might be Ezekiel. If it is, tell him I'll be up there in a minute," she yelled.

"OK."

"Who is it?"

"It's Ezekiel."

Maniya opened the door and saw him standing there looking well rested, clean and ready to console her friend.

"Come in Ezekiel. How are you?"

"I'm well and you?"

"I've been better, let me get Shar for you."

"How is she?"

"Well given the circumstances, as well as she can be. I hate seeing her like this. We're hoping for the best, you know?"

"Yeah, I'm glad I can be here to help out anyway I can."

"Thank you for that, it truly says a lot. Let me go get her."

Shar was putting the last of her belongings in her suitcase when Maniya entered the room.

"Maniya I'm sorry I have to leave early. Thank you so much for everything.

"Shar please, I definitely understand. We have plenty of time to resume. Right now you need to get home with your family."

"I know, it just came out of nowhere; things were going great."

"Speaking of great, there is a great gentleman in my living room waiting for you."

A smile emerged through the gloom on Shar's face.

"Was that Ezekiel at the door?"

"Yes it was."

"OK, I think I have everything."

"Awww, give me a hug. I love you. Everything is going to be fine, keep the faith lady."

"I will. Thank you and I love you too. I'll call you once I know what flight I'll be on."

"Sounds good. Give your mom and dad my love."

"Will do."

Shar grabbed her bags and walked toward the living room and Maniya followed her.

"Hey Ezekiel."

Ezekiel stood up to greet Shar and gave her a hug.

"Hey, are you all ready to go?"

"Yeah, I have to get the next flight out to Orlando."

"Orlando? I thought your parents lived in Palm Coast."

"They do but he's being airlifted to Florida Hospital."

"I'll let you fill me in later. We can see about changing your flight in the car. Let me get those bags and get you to the airport."

"Thanks again Manny. I'll call you as soon as I know something and Ezekiel thank you for coming."

"Not a problem, I'm glad I can be here for you."

"I hate leaving like this."

"Don't do that, your family needs you; that's where you need to be right now. We can always pick up where we left off; I'm not worried about that."

Shar looked at Ezekiel and her heart fluttered.

"You are remarkable."

They got in the car and Ezekiel headed for JFK.

"Try to call and see what flights are available."

"I pray there's a direct flight leaving within the hour that I can take. It is going to take at least two hours."

"It will work out, don't worry."

"I'm on hold right now, come on people," said Shar almost in a panic.

"So you finally talked to your mom?"

"Yes, she called as I was getting out of the shower. She told me that my dad was in a diabetic coma, that's why I got to get there."

"I'm sorry to hear that. How's your mom holding up?"

"She sounds okay. She's always trying to be a rock, but you never know how she's feeling beneath the surface."

"I know what you mean. My father died when I was young and I don't think I ever saw my mom cry."

Shar shook her head in disbelief. "It's amazing how they exhibit so much strength. Tears love falling from my eyes. I'm sorry to hear about your loss at a young age."

"Thank you. It wasn't easy but we made it through."

"Hello. Hello. I don't believe this. The call dropped."

Ezekiel reached for Shar's hand and told her not to worry about it.

"I think that is easier said than done."

"I'll make a call and have you on a plane when we get there."

"How are you going to manage that?"

"My jet is on standby."

Shar cleared her throat as she looked in Ezekiel's direction. She didn't want to seem too shocked that Ezekiel just mentioned, ever so casually, that he had his jet on stand-by. So she collected her thoughts and said okay as calmly as she could.

"I'll call in so they can notify the pilot and he'll have you in Orlando in a few hours."

Ezekiel makes the call to get everything cleared and Shar looks at her phone to check the time.

"Lord please let everything work out and thank you for not letting me be alone right now," said Shar silently in prayer.

"Everything is set. The pilot will be ready to go when we get there; we are about 10 minutes away."

"Thank you so much, from the bottom of my heart."

Ezekiel reached out his right hand and connected it with Shar's left hand.

"Don't mention it. Keep the faith and know that everything will work out for the best."

"I will. Let me call my mom and Manny before I board."

Shar called her mom first, but her call went straight to voicemail.

"Mom, it's Shar. I'm about to get on a plane. I should be in Orlando around 7:15 or so. I love you and tell dad I send my love too. See you soon."

Ezekiel focused on the road as he approached the airport entrance.

"Hey Manny."

"Hey Shar."

"I just wanted to call you to let you know that I'm about to get on a plane."

"OK great."

"I should be in Orlando around 7:15."

"What's your flight number?"

"I don't have one; I couldn't get my flight changed but Ezekiel arranged for me to get there on his private jet."

"Private jet?"

"Yes," she said, managing to hold back the scream she would've released if Ezekiel wasn't in her presence. "God always provides."

"Yes he does, yes he does. Magnify his name honey because he surely is blessing you abundantly."

"Manny I will talk to you when I get there."

"OK, bye. Have a safe flight."

"Bye Manny." "That girl is something else," said Shar with a smile.

Ezekiel parked the car and opened the door for Shar before getting her bags out of the back. He walked her over to his jet and introduced her to Rick, his pilot. There was a flight attendant accompanying them as well and she took Shar's bags in to stow them away.

"Mr. E will you be joining us in flight?"

"No Rick, I won't but please report when you land in Orlando."

"Not a problem, will do sir."

"Wonderful."

Ezekiel gave Shar a long, strong hug and told her to keep him posted.

"I will," said Shar.

"Call me if you need anything."

Shar boarded the plane and sat down in the plush leather chair.

"Good evening ma'am, my name is Sarah. Can I get you something refreshing to drink?"

Shar almost asked for something strong to ease her mind but she opted for a bottle of water instead. She buckled her seat belt and closed her eyes to pray for a safe flight and when she opened her eyes, Sarah was back with a chilled bottle of water and a glass.

"Here you are ma'am. I also brought you some fresh fruit and mixed nuts."

"Thank you very much and please call me Shar."

Rick announced that the plane was cleared to depart and reminded them to stay seated and buckled in until they reached a certain altitude.

"It is 5:15 now; we should be arriving in Orlando around 7:45. Skies are clear, so we have a nice smooth ride in store for us. Enjoy!"

Shar checked her phone; no missed calls or messages. She held it tightly and closed her eyes and silently prayed, "God please restore my father's strength."

The plane was accelerating on the runway and in moments, it started ascending.

Chapter 14

A Little Later

Rick could not have timed the flight any better. They arrived at the Orlando International Airport at 7:45 P.M. on the dot. Shar sent a text to Maniya and Ezekiel to let them know she arrived safely. After she got off the plane, she thanked Rick and Sarah, got her belongings and to her surprise, Ezekiel had a car waiting to take her to the hospital. The driver greeted Shar and held the door open until she was seated. He took her bags and stored them in the trunk.

"We are all set, but just to clarify; you're going to Florida Hospital, right?"

"Yes, that's correct."

"I'll have you there in about 20 minutes."

"OK, thank you."

Shar tried to make herself comfortable in the car before she called her mom to let her know she was in route to the hospital.

"Hello."

"Mom?"

"Hey Shar," said her mom tiredly.

"I'm here in Orlando, on the way to the hospital. How's dad? How are you?"

"I'm well baby, with God's grace, I can't complain. Your dad is still in a coma, they are trying to stabilize his vitals."

Shar sighed, relieved that her mom was holding up well but disappointed that her father was still in a coma.

"Manny sends her love."

"She's still a sweetheart."

"Yeah, she's still Manny. Mom what room is dad in?"

"It's room D222. When you get here go through the emergency wing, it'll be easier to access."

"OK. Do you need anything? Have you eaten?

"No I haven't eaten, but I can't eat."

"Mom you have to eat something, I can't have both of you sick now. I'll see you in a little while. I love you."

"I love you too baby. See you soon."

Shar took a deep breath and called out to the driver, "Excuse me."

"Yes ma'am."

"Can you stop by a Panera or Wendy's near the hospital please?"

"Sure can, which one? They are both near it."

"Wendy's may be quicker."

"Will do."

"Thanks."

Shar arrived at the hospital within an hour of landing at the airport. The driver informed her that Ezekiel reserved the car for the entire evening, so she did not have to drag her bags inside. She looked upward and moved her lips to say thank you God without volume.

Shar grabbed the food and her purse and exited the car.

"Thank you kindly," she told the driver. Let me get your business card so I can call you before I come out."

"Yes ma'am. My name is Johnathan McDaniel and my number is on the back of this card."

"Great."

"I hope everything is OK," said Johnathan sincerely as he watched Shar walk into the sliding door of the hospital.

Shar didn't care for hospitals because she always got an eerie feeling when she visited one. She never quite understood why but it was something about them. She checked off a long list in her mind as she walked the halls: they were always frigid inside, the constant beeps in rooms, strange people all about, quiet halls, stale colored walls, unpleasant smells and the fact that the last time she saw her grandmothers alive, was in a hospital bed.

"OK Shar, get it together, be strong for pops," she thought.

She found the elevator and went to the 2nd floor.

The signs on the wall in front of her read Rooms D201-D211 ← and Rooms D212-D222 →. Shar went to the right and her father's room was a few steps down the hall on the left. The door was slightly ajar and Shar went in. Her mom was sitting in a recliner next to Shar's father with a bible nestled in her hands. Shar wanted to cry when she saw her father laying in that narrow bed practically lifeless. There were so many monitors and cords connected to him, she almost didn't recognize him.

"Mom," Shar called out.

"Shar baby, you made it."

She couldn't get out the chair fast enough to greet Shar and hug her tightly.

"Oh I'm so glad you're here. I want your dad to see your smiling face when he wakes up," said her mom as she squeezed Shar.

"You look great mom."

"Thank you honey, I try but I must say; you are gorgeous. I wonder where you got your looks," she said with a smirk on her face.

"Mom please," Shar said with laughter. "You always know how to make me feel better at times like this."

"Honey if there's one thing I have learned in life, it definitely is laughing beats crying."

"I can't stand to see dad looking like this, you know that and on top of that, I wasn't there for you when it happened."

Shar walked over to her father and kissed him on the forehead.

"Hey daddy, it's your baby girl, Shar. "You have to wake up now, enough is enough." She couldn't hold back the tears any longer. "Daddy if you can hear me, I love you. Mom and I love you so much and we're scared. We need you to find your strength and come back. Let our love for you and your love for us guide you back daddy, please."

Shar's mom came beside her and wiped the tears from her eyes with a tissue and guided her to a chair.

"Come on baby, he hears you. I know it's hard to see him this way but he's going to come back to us. Come on sit down, what did you bring in this bag?"

Sniffling and drying a few remaining tears, Shar managed to say, "I almost forgot that I stopped at Wendy's to get us a bite to eat. I got you a Jr. Bacon Cheeseburger and a side salad."

"Thank you, but you didn't have to do that."

"Mom you have to eat something."

"Yes ma'am."

"Have the doctors told you anything since he's been here?"

She nodded yes as she chewed the bite of sandwich.

"They are hopeful and that's good. They said if he had gone unnoticed for much longer it would be a different story."

"Thank God you went back into the house when you did. I'm sorry you were by yourself when it happened though. I wish I could have been there with you."

"It was scary. It took everything in me not to panic. God gave me the strength I needed and steered my mind in the right direction."

"Have you called Uncle Klay and Auntie Mae?"

"No I haven't."

"Mom, you have to call them, they're his siblings."

"I know, I will. I was just hoping that he would be out of the coma by now."

"What about a hotel room, did you get one?"

'No I will be right here."

"Were you able to bring a change of clothes?"

"No baby."

"Well I have a car downstairs that's waiting for me. I'm going to go get a room at a hotel nearby and go get you a few items from Wal-Mart and come back."

"Sounds good, we'll be here."

Shar kissed her mom on the cheek and walked over to her father, kissed him on the cheek and whispered in his ear, "I'll be back soon. I love you." "I love you mom, see you in a few."

"OK."

Shar headed down the hall to the elevator. She pulled out her phone and Johnathan's phone number.

"Hey Johnathan, it's Shar. I'm headed down."

"I'm pulling up to the front now."

"Thank you."

Shar asked Johnathan to take her up the road to the Comfort Suite to get a room. She took her bags in and washed her face quickly before going back down to the car where Johnathan was waiting like she requested.

"You have truly been a God-send, thank you so much for your patience," she said to him.

"You're welcome ma'am."

"I need to go to Wal-Mart. Is there one nearby?"

"Yes, there's one a few miles from here."

"Great. I have to pick up a couple of things to bring back to the hospital and that will be all I need tonight."

"You got it."

Shar went into Wal-Mart and tried to stay focused on what she was in there for. She ran down a mental list: a few dresses, underwear, flats, and toiletries for mom. "There that should do it for mom. I need some fruit and blank thank you cards. Get those things and get out of here Shar," she thought. She went through the store making sure to gather all the items on her mental list. Before she knew it, she was in the checkout line with a bag of Dove chocolates, white cheddar popcorn, orange juice, a beautiful small Birds of Paradise plant and everything on her mental list.

"How are you this evening? Did you find everything you needed?" the clerk asked.

"I'm great, thank you for asking. Yes, I found everything I came for and some extras."

"That's how it happens most of the time," said the clerk with a smile. Shar paid for her items and pushed the cart of bags to the car.

Johnathan helped her put the bags in the car.

"Thank you," she said.

On the way back to the hospital Shar mentioned that she would probably have to make two trips to the room with the bags and apologized in advance for any inconvenience.

"No ma'am, there will be no need for that; I'll help you with the bags. You just make sure that beautiful plant gets to its destination safely." "You are a gem, thank you again. I will definitely let Ezekiel know about the great service you have extended to me."

"It has been my pleasure ma'am."

Johnathan pulled up at the hospital and parked. He helped Shar out of the car, grabbed the bags and followed her lead to her father's room. Shar went in the room to put the plant down then returned to the hall to get the bags from Johnathan.

"I can't say thank you enough. Have a great night and enjoy," she said as she gave him a $100 bill.

"Oh ma'am thank you but I can't accept that. Mr. Ezekiel has already paid me generously."

"I insist," said Shar as she began to turn away.

"Thank you. If you need my services anymore while you're here, don't hesitate to call. Good night."

Johnathan walked away and Shar re-entered her father's room. Her dad was still lying there connected to machines and her mom had nodded off on the recliner. Shar placed the bags down and went over to kiss her father on the forehead.

"I'm back daddy," she whispered. "I brought you something but you have to wake up to see it; the Birds of Paradise plant was his favorite. He loved how it bloomed and he had them planted about at home. She walked over to her mom and kissed her on the cheek.

"I'm back ma," she whispered.

Her mom squirmed a little and opened her eyes.

"Baby what time is it?"

"It's a little passed 11:00."

"Hmmm. Did you get everything situated?"

"Yes ma'am. I checked into a room and I went by Wal-Mart and grabbed some undergarments and things for you as well as some snacks." "Aww, thanks baby," said Mrs.Belle.

"Don't mention it mama, it's the least I can do."

Her mom smiled at her as she took the garments and toiletries out of the bag.

"Look at that beautiful plant. Bird of Paradise; your father is going to love it."

"I know right. I saw it and couldn't leave the store without it."

"Are you coming back to the room with me to shower and get some proper rest?"

"Oh no, I'm staying right here. I'm going to take a shower here, put this gown on and sleep right here next to your father."

"I knew that, I'm not sure why I asked that stupid question. I'll wait here while you shower and then I'll get a taxi to the hotel and come back in the morning."

"I should just be a few minutes."

"Don't rush mama; I'm not in a hurry."

Her mom took what she needed in the bathroom and showered.

"My goodness what a day," said Shar as she reclined in the chair and glanced over at her dad.

"Hey daddy, your baby girl is tired. I wish you would open your eyes or smile for me. It would surely give my energy levels a boost. Hey guess what? You know how you have been at me lately about finding a good man and starting a family, right? I think heaven has finally smiled down on me with someone. Yep, his name is Ezekiel. Something about his name alone is powerful to me. He owns a financial firm with his brother. He's very handsome and kind, and he's quite the gentleman. I met him at an island club when I was out with Manny and we danced together through a number of songs. I really think that if you meet him, you'd like him daddy. He's very ambitious and he's the reason I was able to get here so fast today. He arranged for his pilot to fly me in on his jet. No kidding; he has a jet but he is the most humble man I think I've ever met, besides you of course. You'll see."

"Shar who are you talking to?"

"I'm just talking to daddy, mama."

"Oh my lord, did he wake up?" she said rushing to his bedside.

"No, no mama not yet, but I'm talking to him just the same. Something tells me he can hear me just fine."

"You know what Shar, I think you're right," she said before leaning over to kiss her husband on the lips and telling him she loved him.

"I'm all set; you can call for your taxi and chat with me for a while until it comes."

"OK."

Shar called for a taxi and the operator told her that a driver would arrive in 15 minutes. Her mom was anxious for her to hang up the phone because she wanted to hear about New York and take her mind off her husband's condition for a moment.

"Are they coming?"

"Yes ma'am, a driver should be here in about 15 minutes."

"Great, so tell me about New York. How was it and how's Manny doing these days?"

"Manny is doing great. She lives in this luxurious apartment on 5th Ave with an immaculate view. We sat out on her balcony and had tea and cocktails several times. We went shopping and out to a few clubs and restaurants. Oh mama, it was absolutely gorgeous. There's this restaurant called DESTINY with such a magnificent ambiance and a menu to match. You and dad definitely have to go there."

"It sounds wonderful Shar. Did you meet anyone interesting?"

"As a matter of fact I did. That's what I was talking to dad about while you were in the shower.

"For real?"

"Yes. I met a guy my first night there but we didn't exchange numbers or anything. I ran into him again when Manny and I were having lunch at DESTINY and he gave me his business card. I called him later that night and we actually went on a double date with Manny and his brother to a hot jazz spot at the Lincoln Center."

Her mom was hanging on her every word, waiting to hear what Shar was going to say next.

"We had a great time. He's quite the gentleman. He doesn't have any kids and he's financially sound. Oh and did I mention how handsome he is?"

"No, but the way you're smiling when you talk about him, I know he has you captivated baby girl."

"Ma, I can't tell you how refreshing it is to have met him. I would not have made it to Orlando without him today."

"Why do you say that?"

"I couldn't get through to the airline in a timely manner and he arranged for me to come here on his jet."

"His jet?"

"Yes, you heard right but listen I have to go down stairs, the taxi should be pulling up in a moment."

"But Shar wait a minute."

"Got to go mom," said Shar as she leaned over to kiss her mom on the cheek and gave her a hug.

"We'll finish talking about New York tomorrow."

Her mom looked at her with slanted eyes and said, "We better. Be safe out there and call me when you get to your room."

"I will, make sure your phone is on. I love you."

"I love you too."

Shar left the room went downstairs and the taxi was waiting for her outside the sliding door. She was in good spirits considering the circumstances. Something in her heart reassured her that everything would be fine.

She opened the door to get in the taxi and paused.

"Ahhh," she said.

"Is everything alright Miss?"

"Yeah, everything is fine. I just left a bag upstairs."

"Well I can wait for you to get it if you need me to."

"No, that won't be necessary, it's just snacks I probably don't need anyway."

"If you say so; you're going to the Comfort Suites up the road, right?"

"You got it."

"My dove chocolate would've been lovely right about now," she thought as she sank into the backseat and gazed out the window.

The ride was short and Shar was exhausted. Shar could see her bed with every step she took inside the hotel. She made it to her room, kicked off her shoes and took her phone out of her purse to charge it.

Two missed calls.

Shar had missed a call from Maniya and Ezekiel.

"Oh my goodness, I forgot to text them and let them know how things were going since I landed. It's too late to call now. I'll just send them a text."

"Hey there. I made it to the hospital. There's no change as of yet with his status but we are still in good spirits. I just got to my room and about to call it a night. I'll call you tomorrow."

She sent that message to Ezekiel and Maniya, skipped her shower and gave into the comfy mattress and plush pillows.

Chapter 15

Monday at Sunrise

The sun peeked through the sheer curtains in Shar's room but she hadn't noticed. She heard a slight noise and turned on her side as if she'd received a long awaited cue. Moments later, she heard the noise again but this time there was a series of knocks. Shar rubbed her eyes and ignored the knocks, but they repeated.

"What the hell?"

"Housekeeping," called out from the other side of the door.

"No come back later."

"No problem ma'am."

"It's too early for housekeeping. It's probably not even 8 o'clock yet."

Shar stretched, rolled over and grabbed her phone off the nightstand. She had texts messages and two missed calls from her mom. To her surprise, it was already 11 o'clock.

"I must've been really tired," she said.

She called her mom to let her know she was OK and just slept late. She figured that was why she called her.

"Hey mom, I saw you called. I just woke up. I'll be there soon."

"Shar good morning, get here as soon as you can baby."

"What's wrong? What's going on?"

"Shar baby, just get here, I'd rather not say over the phone."

"But mom?"

"I love you baby."

"Shit. God please, I'm sorry. I just don't have time for this now. Please let my dad be fine, please."

Shar stared in the mirror contemplating on taking a shower or just hailing a cab with what she had on; morning breath and all. She needed to get to the hospital as soon as possible. She took a deep breath and remembered that her parents raised her better. Under no circumstances should she go out in public looking thrown away. Besides, there may be good news waiting for her so she was going to be ready for it.

She took a shower, teased her hair and put on a dress that resembled a Bird of Paradise. She looked stunning and felt great. Now she was ready to face whatever awaited her at the hospital. She hailed a taxi in front of the hotel.

"Where to?"

"Florida Hospital, please."

"You got it beautiful."

Shar leaned back in the seat of the taxi and closed her eyes. She was trying to remain calm and think of the great times she shared with her parents. She looked at her phone to check the time. It was close to noon and her phone still showed unread text messages.

"You and your family are in my prayers Shar. Stay strong, God is going to work it all out. I'm here for you. Love Manny."

Shar placed her right hand over her heart as she read the message.

Hey Shar. Thanks for keeping me updated. If there is anything I can do for you or your family, let me know. I'll be thinking of you and keeping you and your family in my prayers. Galvi sends his regards as well Ttyl. Ezekiel.

Shar was so taken by their words she didn't realize that she was at the hospital. She gave the driver his fare and exited the vehicle.

As she walked through the halls of the frigid hospital, she couldn't help but notice the other patients and their family members occupying space. Some of them were expressionless while others were in tears. She could feel their pain in every step, praying that God would heal their bodies and hearts along the way.

"Lord while you are at it, please strengthen me. I don't know what's waiting on the other side of this door," she said just before she entered her father's room.

She turned the knob and heard laughter, "ta he he he," echoed the room.

"Daddy," Shar whispered. Why she chose to whisper is unbeknown to her.

"Shar, you made it," said her mom.

"Did I just hear daddy laughing or is my mind playing tricks on me?"

"Baby girl," a voice called out panting. "You heard right. Come give your daddy a hug."

"Oh daddy," she said ecstatically with her eyes wide and bright and a smile that extended from one ear to the other.

"Thank God, oh thank God. You had me scared to death and mom rushed me here and wouldn't tell me what was going on."

She hugged her father tightly trying not to hurt him as he still had an IV connected to him.

"I couldn't let my baby girl down. Thank you for the plant, it's almost as beautiful as you and your mother."

"Daddy please."

If Shar could climb in the bed with him she would but she had to settle for holding his hand and standing by his bedside.

"Baby I'm sorry for keeping you in suspense but I wanted you to see for yourself how great

God is. He is not 100% yet of course but he's awake and alert and the doctor says it is nothing short of a miracle."

"I'll be out of here in no time."

"You better be," said Shar. "And don't you dare scare us like this again."

"Yes ma'am," he replied.

"Daddy, you have to do better and take care of yourself! Diabetes is nothing to take lightly."

"I know, I promise you that I will do better."

He took her hand and kissed it gently.

"What were you laughing about earlier anyhow?"

"Your mom and I were watching *Sanford and Son*."

"Oh, say no more! I know that's one of your favorite shows that keeps you laughing."

"Yeah, Redd Fox was one of the best."

The phone started to ring in the room just as the show came back on.

"Hello."

"Hey Mae."

"Yes, God is able. We're doing fine. Shar just came in."

"Yes, of course. Shar your Aunt Mae says hello."

"Hey auntie," replied Shar loud enough for her to hear.

"Baby, it's your sister," she said as she handed the phone over breaking his attention from the television.

Shar whispered to her mom, "I'm going to step out for a minute. I'm so happy to see daddy's eyes and hear him talking. This is wonderful. I'll be right back."

Shar stepped in the hall and called Ezekiel. While the phone was ringing, she felt a tap on her shoulder. She turned around to find a doctor's coat standing in front of her. Her eyes scanned upward and when she saw his face, she heard two voices calling her name. She expected to hear Ezekiel answering her call but she was not prepared to see Dexter, her ex standing in front of her.

She didn't know whether to faint or go blind as Aunt Mae would say.

"Shar?"

"Yes Ezekiel," she replied to the voice on the phone while putting her finger up to Dexter before she turned and walked away.

"It's so good to hear your voice. How is everything?"

"Everything is wonderful. My daddy is up and looking good, that's why I called you."

"That's outstanding Shar. God does answer prayers, doesn't he?"

"He surely does. How are you doing?"

"I'm great. I'm actually in Miami right now handling a little business."

"Really?"

"Yeah, I was going to stop by your hotel and surprise you but I didn't want to appear stalkerish," said Ezekiel with a chuckle.

"Stalkerish, now why would you say that?"

"I'm just saying. I know it seems like I've known you forever but I haven't. It hasn't even been a week, but I feel a great connection with you and I don't want to ruin it by doing something stupid."

"Ezekiel, I can't imagine you doing anything stupid. You have done so much for me already. I don't know how to begin to repay you."

"Now that is one thing you don't have to worry about. Anything I do for you is from my heart; there's nothing to repay."

"How long are you going to be in Miami?"

"I like how you changed the subject without acknowledging what I said, but I meant it."

"I hear you and I got it, now tell me how long you're going to be in Miami."

"I'm not sure yet, no later than Friday I presume. Don't worry if I can't steal away some time to come see you before going back home. I'd like to make that happen though."

Shar was blushing hard. She wondered if only he knew how he had her wrapped around his fingers.

"Well that would be great. I don't know how long they plan on keeping my dad here but prayerfully he'll be returning home soon."

"I'm sure he will babe... Shar," he said quickly correcting himself.

"Thank you."

"Beep," sounded Shar's phone signaling another call coming in.

"Ezekiel, I have a call coming in from Manny. Let me get it and I'll talk to you a little later today."

"Sounds good. I'll talk to you then."

"Bye."

"Hey Manny."

"Hi Shar, how are you?"

"I'm great. My dad is awake, thank God. My mom's good, I just talked to Ezekiel and guess who I saw a few minutes ago?"

"Wait a minute Shar, your dad is out of the coma?"

"Yes, yes, yes!" she said with great excitement.

"That's a beautiful blessing, I'm so glad to hear that. I know you mom is glowing."

"You know it, me too. He gave us quite a scare girl."

"I know. How's Ezekiel?"

"He's good. He is actually in Miami on business for a few days."

"He seems to have his stuff together Shar. I think he's a keeper, you think?"

"I know right and Manny, his jet, oh my God."

"Honey say no more, I can only imagine. Hmmh, hmmh, hmmh."

"How are you and his brother doing?"

"Fine. We went back to Dizzy's the other night. You would be proud of me."

"What do you mean?"

"We haven't had sex yet."

"Get the freak out of here! You're kidding right?"

"No I'm serious. We had a great time enjoying conversation and each other, but nothing else besides a little kissing."

"What?"

"Yes, and if the kissing is any implication of how it's going to be when we're one, have mercy."

"Manny, you are crazy girl and you're right, I'm proud of you. Hell you just might be onto something special here, you think?"

"Not sure but it feels good. Did I tell you that crazy ex of mine is still calling trying to see me?"

"Chile, change your number, just make sure I get the new one."

"I know. I just don't understand what he could possibly want."

"To get on your nerves if you let him. Hell I almost forgot, guess who was standing in front of me with scrubs and a doctor's coat on?"

"Who?"

"You're not going to believe this."

"Who Shar?"

"If I told you, you wouldn't believe me."

"Shar."

"Girl, Dexter."

"Dexter, Dexter? Get the hell out of here."

"I kid you not."

"So he finally completed something huh? What did he say? Did you talk to him?"

"No, not yet. I had Ezekiel on the phone in one ear and he was standing in front of me calling my name. I chose to talk to Ezekiel and motioned my finger to him to give me a moment."

"Shar you are something fierce."

"I don't have time for foolery. Dexter was and as far as I know, is about those games and I don't have room for that in my life anymore.

"You know you don't have to tell me twice."

"He looked good though, that I have to say. My lord, he looked good."

"Like that?"

"Yes ma'am, like that. I was tempted to touch but I didn't."

"So are you going to talk to him?"

"I don't know, I wonder if he knows why I'm here. You think he knows my dad is a patient here?"

"That's a good question, but you can easily find out."

"You're right. Well, let me get back in there with my parents. They're probably wondering where I ran off to anyway."

"Cool, we'll talk soon."

"Indeed, bye."

"Bye."

Shar placed her phone in her back pocket, glanced in the mirror hanging in the corner by the double doors in the hall, patted her hair and puckered her lips as if she was giving her reflection a kiss.

"Okay," she said to herself as she walked back toward her father's room. She opened the door and she was greeted by laughter again. This time there was more laughter and it wasn't coming from the television.

"Shar, where have you been? I tried calling you. Your father's doctor is here making his rounds. He says your father is doing fine."

"Would you give her a minute to answer you? My goodness," said Shar's father.

"It's okay daddy really."

"You know how he is Shar."

"Well I'm glad you are doing great daddy. Where's the doctor anyhow?"

"Oh he had to go in the restroom to wash his face; your daddy had him crying laughing imitating Fred Sanford and Ester."

"Oh lord. Daddy really?"

"Well I've got to have a little fun while I still can."

"You sure do," said Shar as she leaned down to give him a kiss.

"Okay, Mr. and Mrs. Belle. Thank you for the laughs and Mr. Belle, keep it up and you'll be out of here in no time."

"Oh my word, it can't be," Shar thought to herself when she heard the voice.

"Have you met my daughter yet?"

"I don't believe I have," said the doctor.

He walked out of the bathroom just as Shar turned to look in his direction.

"Baby girl, this is Dr. Harris. He saved your daddy's life."

Shar and Dexter locked eyes and they both hesitated to say hello again. Shar wasn't ready to introduce Dexter to her family when they were dating and she sure as hell didn't want them to know who he was now. This is the same guy who strung her along for 5 years because he didn't have the decency to divorce his wife or just let Shar be.

"Lord please don't let this fool act like he knows me, it's not the time nor the place to explain to my parents that this is the infamous mystery man that put me through so much hell," she thought.

"Nice to meet you," she said. "Thank you so much for taking care of my father."

Dexter stood before her with a look of confusion. "Nice to meet you too," he said. His thought was, "Is she crazy? After all of those sleepless nights and days we had with endless conversations and passionate rendezvous in between the sheets, nice to meet you?"

Shar could feel the tension in every breath Dexter took, so she eased her way over to her mother and kissed her on the cheek.

"So mama, are you excited about getting this fine young man to the house?"

Her mother looked at her with a smirk on her face and said, "Which one, the doctor or your father?" Everyone laughed and Shar tapped her mom on the shoulder. "Really mama?"

"Well they're both fine young men."

"You guys are great but I have some rounds to make. Have a great night everyone."

"Goodnight," replied Mr. and Mrs. Belle, Shar smirked gently and nodded in agreement.

Chapter 16

Good Evening

Shar stared at the door as if part of her wanted to run out there after Dexter but she knew better. Her mom noticed her blank stare and called out to her, "Shar. Shar. Are you okay?"

"Yes mama I'm fine," she said still gazing at the door.

"He is a fine young man, it's too bad he has a wedding band on," said her mom.

"If you only knew," murmured Shar.

"What did you say?"

"Oh nothing mama."

"Alright, alright enough of that foolishness. Y'all are going to act like I'm a man in this room now here," said her father.

"That's right daddy, get her."

Shar's mom looked at them sideways, patted her hair and rolled her eyes playfully.

"Baby you know you are the only one for me," she said as she walked over to him to give him a kiss on his forehead, then his nose and finishing on his lips.

Shar smiled enjoying the display of love and affection that her parents have shared for nearly 40 years.

"How sweet," she said, "I love you guys."

"And we love you," said her mom as she nose- wrestled with her husband.

"Enough already, you guys are going to make me cry."

"Well it's the truth baby."

"I know, I know. It feels good to be loved by the best parents ever."

There was a light knock on the door before it was gently pushed open.

"Good evening Mr. Belle. I hope you're ready to eat this wonderful meal."

Shar's father shook his head in disbelief. There was no way in the world any meal in a hospital could be good he thought.

"Yum, yum," said the nurse.

"Yeah right, what is this?"

"Chicken broth soup sir and a little apple sauce."

"I'm not eating this crap," he said.

"Daddy you have to eat something or you can't be released to go home."

He shook his head and grunted, looking away from his tray.

"Try it baby, it might surprise you," encouraged Mrs. Belle.

"Yeah, it'll surprise me alright, right back into a coma," he said before reluctantly taking a sip of the soup. His expression changed slightly when he realized it wasn't entirely tasteless and he took another sip.

"See daddy, it's not that bad, right?"

"Eh now, it's not your mother's cooking."

"Well we know that."

"You'll have my cooking soon enough; you just have to eat this in the meantime."

He continued sipping away at the soup until it was practically gone while Shar and her mother watched him lovingly just as if he was an infant eating a meal with his fingers for the first time.

"Daddy you are something else. I'm about to go, I need to eat something myself. Mom do you need anything before I go back to the hotel?"

"No baby, I'm fine. Will you be back in the morning?"

"Yes ma'am. I need to get home and get back to work too, my vacation is over."

"Back to work, don't they know I'm in the hospital?"

"Yes daddy they do but you're doing better now. Once I know you and mom are well and back home, I have to get back to work."

"Yeah, yeah, yeah."

"Oh stop it old man," said Mrs. Belle.

"I love you both, see you tomorrow."

Shar walked down the hall toward the elevator and it dawned on her that she didn't call a taxi. Hoping that she would find a vacant taxi waiting when she got downstairs, she continued. She walked outside and there was not a taxi in sight, just the still of the night. The sky was dark with a few sparkles from the stars and a subtle glow from the new moon. Shar reached in her purse for her phone and at that moment she felt a gentle tap on her shoulder. She jumped.

"Shar it's me, Dexter. I didn't mean to startle you. I noticed you standing out here alone. Are you okay?"

"I'm fine. I was just about to call a taxi."

"You don't have to do that. I just ended my shift. I can take you wherever you need to go."

"I don't know about that. I've heard that before."

"Come on Shar; give me a break will you. I'm a better man than I used to be but you won't give me a chance to show you."

"Really Dex, says the man who's still wearing his wedding band."

"Dex, wow I missed hearing you call me that. I didn't know what to say when you acted like you didn't know me in front of your parents."

"Why should I have responded differently?"

"We had some great moments through the years."

"Yeah and don't forget about as many, if not more, not so great moments too."

"I don't want to think about those moments."

"I bet you don't. Just as you don't want to think about the fact that you are still married, yet you are out here bothering me. Just go Dexter, I'll be fine."

"I'm not leaving you out here Shar."

"But Dexter I am no longer your concern darling."

Shar dialed the number to the taxi company.

"Hello."

"Hi, yes, how soon can you have a taxi to Florida Hospital?"

"I can have a driver there for you in about 25 minutes at best," said the dispatcher.

"25 minutes?"

"Yes ma'am."

"See Shar there's no wait if you let me take you. Have you eaten yet?"

Shar turned around and found Dexter still standing there.

"You're still here?"

"Excuse me," replied the lady on the phone.

"My apologies miss, I was speaking to someone else. You can cancel the call."

"Have a great evening."

"I will, do the same. Goodbye."

"Okay Dexter, you can take me to grab a bite to eat before dropping me off at my hotel. In return I will listen to whatever it is you have to say while you're driving."

"Deal."

"And don't try to take any scenic routes. Find the nearest Chili's and park curbside to go. I just want some wings and a side salad."

"What about me? You don't want to eat inside?"

"No, I'm spending too much time with you as it is and shouldn't your wife have dinner waiting for you when you get home?"

Dexter didn't say a word. He unlocked the car and opened Shar's door like a perfect gentleman.

"Thank you," said Shar as she entered the car and buckled up.

"Lord please give my friend the strength to fight the temptation in front of her," said Maniya as she began to close her eyes while stretched out on the couch. It was as if she had an emotional detector on Shar or something.

They did almost everything together and they knew each other through and through. Besides, Maniya knew more than anyone how head over heels Shar was about Dexter. If she knew any better though, she would be asking the Lord for some strength of her own as well.

Chapter 17

Late Evening

There were a series of knocks at Maniya's door.

"Who in the world could this be?" she thought as she started to get off the couch.

The knocks at the door were repeated.

Maniya didn't say a word before she looked through the peep hole. She looked but no one was there.

"Who is it?" she asked.

There was no reply.

"Who is it?" she asked again.

Still, no reply.

She opened the door and to her surprise there was an oversized bouquet of white roses in front of her door with a card attached.

Sorry for stopping by unannounced but I needed to see your smile. If you would grant me the honor, I'll be waiting in the lobby.

Maniya picked up the roses and placed them on the counter. She couldn't believe that Galvi would go through all of this but if this is what he wanted, she decided she would play along.

Maniya quickly washed her face, brushed her teeth and slipped on some clothes. She hurried down stairs to the lobby, smiling from ear to ear, carrying one of the white roses. She looked about the room, but Galvi was nowhere in sight. When she turned around to go back to her place, Deran was standing in front of her. Maniya's smile quickly dropped, along with her rose.

"What are you doing here? How did you find me?" she gasped.

"I have my ways Maniya, I've never stopped loving you, why can't you hear me out?"

"I tried to hear your tired ass out over and over again for almost 5 years Deran."

He gazed into her eyes but couldn't quite make a rebuttal.

"Through all your business trips, late nights and postponed wedding dates, I, Maniya, the one you so-called loved so much, heard your tired ass out. I heard you loud and clear, believed you and loved you more than you deserved! And for what?"

"Baby please."

"Oh yeah, to find out that the baby you wanted to have so badly was born a week after we met."

"Maniya," said Deran as he reached out and grabbed her. She brushed him off and continued, "Let's see, oh yeah, to make matters worse you were planning a wedding with me that you had no intention of following through with because you were already married!"

"You never let me explain Maniya."

"Oh but I did and I heard you too. You loved your tired ass self, more than you loved me, your wife and your child. But I'm good and I hope you are too."

"Baby are you with someone? Can you give me another chance?"

Maniya couldn't help but laugh.

"Another chance Deran? You can't be serious, and please stop calling me baby."

"I never loved her like I love you Maniya and that's the truth. We had something really special."

"No Deran, what we had was a lie that truth destroyed and I couldn't be more grateful."

Maniya stepped closer to Deran, took him by the hand and held it for a moment.

"Thank you for helping me realize that I needed to love myself more than I could expect another person to love me. All is forgiven and I wish you well. There is no room in my life for you now or ever again. I wish you well, take care."

Deran's eyes were welling up but anger won the battle.

As Maniya turned to walk away, he grabbed her arm forcefully and pulled her close to him.

"I can't let you walk away from me like that," said Deran disturbingly.

Maniya tried to remain calm but she was shaken by his actions

"Lord what is wrong with him? Please bring him back to his senses," said Maniya internally.

"Let me go Deran. What has come over you? I don't owe you anything but forgiveness and I gave you that. Let me go."

Deran squeezed her arm a little tighter staring at her with hurt and anger in his eyes.

"You're hurting me, let go," said Maniya a little louder looking down at her wrist.

"I don't think you understand Maniya, I'm not letting you go that easily."

"Right now, I don't think you have a choice brother," said a masculine voice behind her.

Deran moved his focused from Maniya to look behind her. Maniya broke away from Deran, turned slightly and saw Galvi standing there tall, chocolate and prepared for battle with muscles bulging for days. She quickly moved to stand behind him.

"Baby, are you okay?" asked Galvi.

Maniya nodded yes.

"Who in the hell are you?" asked Deran as he stepped forward.

"The man who's thankful that you fucked up years ago and allowed me to be the man you couldn't be."

Maniya's heart fell to the ground as she listened to Galvi speak.

"Is that so?"

"It is and if I heard her correctly, so did you. There's no need for you to be here."

Galvi began to step closer to Deran.

"If I ever see you lay a hand, hell breathe the same air she's breathing, it will be the last breath you take, feel me?"

Deran, a little intimidated by the three extra inches and numerous muscles in Galvi's stature, backed away and left.

Galvi turned around to face Maniya and gently reached out to tilt her head up.

"Are you sure you're okay?"

"Yes, I'm just glad you came by when you did."

"So am I. That was your ex you were telling me about?"

"Unfortunately," she said somberly. "Hey thank you for saying those things to get rid of him."

"That wasn't the only reason I said it, I meant every word."

He gazed into Maniya's eyes as if he saw heaven and kissed her with great passion.

Maniya could have melted in that very spot but somehow she managed to lead Galvi to the elevator without their tongues separating. Maniya's phone started to ring when they got on the elevator but she ignored it. She was enthralled by the chemistry erupting and she didn't want any interruption.

"Where are you Manny?" asked Shar quietly as she waited in the car while Dexter paid for gas.

She pressed 'End Call' on her phone and gazed out of the window at the stars with a look of concern on her face.

"Okay, all set," said Dexter as he got in the car.

"You still want to go to Chili's? If not, there's a great little intimate spot up the road that serves some killer seafood," he said.

"Dexter I'd rather not."

"It was just a suggestion; I know how much you like seafood."

Shar gave him that stare as to say "boy please" and then replied, "Just go to Chili's and I'll order my wings."

Dexter threw his hands up to surrender and drove Shar to Chili's like she requested. He pulled in a curbside parking spot and within moments a gentleman came out and took Shar's order. While they were waiting, Dexter didn't hesitate to lay on a thick apology.

"Shar I have to tell you how much I care about you and how much I valued having you in my life. I apologize from the depth of my soul for my wrongdoings and mistakes that I made when you were with me."

Shar turned to look in his direction and attempted to say something but he wouldn't let her.

"Wait, let me finished please," he said.

Shar looked at him as if he had lost his mind, but she conceded and listened to what he had to say.

"I know I was wrong for dragging you along in my mess, but a part of me needed you and I didn't know how to tell the truth."

Shar sighed as if to say in that deep breath what she was thinking, "Really? Come on now, you can do better than that."

"Shar I wouldn't have finished medical school without your encouragement. You saw something in me that I didn't see in myself and that meant, hell it still means a lot to me."

Shar started to say something but Dexter stopped her again.

"I just want to say thank you and even if you want nothing to do with me, I want you to know that I love you and I always have and always will, and for the record, I'm not married anymore."

At that moment the gentleman returned to the car with Shar's food. Dexter attempted to pay for her meal but Shar refused. She took out a twenty dollar bill to pay and advised the young man to keep the change.

Dexter put the car in reverse and started driving toward Shar's hotel. There was awkward silence in the car and Dexter was waiting on Shar to respond to the things he just said. Instead, Shar gazed out of the window until Dexter got closer to the hotel.

"Thank you for apologizing Dexter. Truth be told, I forgave you a long time ago. Thank you for the credit of helping you realize your abilities. If I didn't, you would not been able to save my father's life. I wish you nothing but the best and I hope that you find love again with the ability to reciprocate it truthfully. What we shared could have been better then, but it is non-existent in the present, with no chance of a future."

Dexter pulled in to the hotel and put the car in park.

"But, Shar listen."

Shar placed a finger over his lips and said, "Shhhhh. It's okay. Thank you for the ride. I wish you nothing but the best available to you. Take care."

She got out of Dexter's car with a smile on her face that could've illuminated the evening sky. She walked through the front door of the hotel and never looked back.

Dexter sat in the car for a moment contemplating running after her, but instead he accepted things for what they were and drove off. Shar couldn't wait to talk to Maniya and tell her what happened, but more importantly, she wanted to hear Ezekiel's voice.

She opened the door, kicked off her shoes and put her food and tote on the table. She started to take her food out the bag and her phone started ringing.

"Hello."

"Hey baby, it's your mom. I just wanted to check to make sure you got in safely."

"Yes ma'am, I just walked through the door."

"Did you get something to eat?"

"I did. I got some wings and I'm about to eat them when I hang up with you."

"Well I won't hold you then."

"No problem mama, how's daddy?"

"He's fine Shar, snoring like no tomorrow. I'm surprised you don't hear him."

Shar laughed and said, "I hope he's not that loud, he'll wake all the patients."

"It's not that bad but anyway good night, enjoy you wings and I'll talk to you tomorrow."

"Ok mama, good night. Love you."

Shar put her phone down and went to wash up before she ate.

"Ooh, I can't wait to dig in to my wings. They smell so good," she said as she washed her hands.

She walked towards the table and her phone rang again. She picked up her phone but she didn't recognize the number.

"Who could this be?"

She looked at her wings and at her phone again and decided to take a bite of a wing before she answered.

"Hello," she said, still chewing a little.

"Hello," said the voice on the other end.

"Shar, I hope I didn't call at a bad time."

"I don't think you could ever do that," she replied.

Ezekiel smiled and paused a moment before replying.

"How was your day? I've been thinking about you and wanting to hear your voice."

"I can't complain, it has been interesting and closing it out talking to you, only makes it better."

"I like the way that sounds. How are your parents?"

"They are doing great. Hopefully my dad gets released tomorrow."

"God is great isn't He?"

"He surely is. How's Miami?"

"It would be better if you were here but I can't complain. Business is great. I'm glad you picked up the phone I know you didn't recognize the number."

"I almost didn't."

"This is my residential line when I'm in Miami. You can store it in your phone so you'll have it because I come down here frequently.

"I'll make sure I do that. So how long will you be there?"

"I wrap up business tomorrow and my plan is to see you before I go home."

"I would love that, I should be home tomorrow and I'm going to see if I can work from home for the rest of the week."

"Sounds great, just let me know. I'm going to get a quick workout in before I go to sleep."

"I will, have a great workout. Good night."

"Good night Shar."

Shar laid her head on her pillow smiled and closed her eyes thinking of how Ezekiel could be the one she'd been waiting for. She forgot about her food, pulled the sheet over her head and went sleep.

Chapter 18

Tuesday Morning Dew

"You are so beautiful, you know that?" Galvi whispered as he stroked Maniya's face. She smiled and continued to melt in his arms.

"I wanted you so bad last night, I could taste every inch of your body on my tongue."

"Well why did you stop? I was more than ready to be your appetizer, main course and dessert."

"Is that so?" he asked while holding her a little tighter.

"Hell yeah. Our chemistry was so intense I was ready to climb the walls with you."

"I don't know, something is telling me to wait. I want to take my time with you. You're different than anyone I've been with lately and I want you to know that this is more than infatuation."

Maniya stared into his eyes trying to wrap her head around what he was saying.

"I want more than sex with you."

"You know that's kind of funny because that goes against everything I've been telling myself I want, but when I'm with you, I feel the same way."

Galvi leaned in to kiss Maniya's lips softly. The passion between them was electrifying. The kiss on the lips led to her neck, down to her breast and he kept going until he kissed every inch of her body. Maniya enjoyed every minute of his gentle touch. He made his way back to her lips and whispered, "Are you ready for me?"

Maniya wrapped her legs around his waist, pulled him in closer, bit him gently on his earlobe and answered, "Yes."

They made love in the morning and enjoyed the afterglow in bed until the mid-afternoon.

Galvi looked into Maniya's eyes and pulled her close to him.

"I don't want this to end."

"That makes two of us."

"If you'll have me, I would love to show you that I meant everything I said earlier."

Maniya leaned in and kissed Galvi on his lips.

"Of course I'll have you, why wouldn't I?"

They kissed and caressed each other a little while longer before getting out of bed. They showered together, ordered in Chinese food and lounged around all day, enjoying the essence of each other.

Chapter 19

Wednesday at Sunset

"Ooh it feels so good to be home," said Shar as she entered her place. It seemed like ages since she'd been home but it was more like a week. She went from New York to Orlando, from Orlando to Daytona and just a few days later than her original plan she was home in Palm Coast. Shar was happy to be home but she was even happier knowing that her dad was home and doing well. It also didn't hurt to know that Ezekiel was as great as she needed him to be.

As she walked about her place, checking on everything and putting her belongings away, she thanked God that everything was in order. She walked into her bedroom and couldn't resist throwing herself across the bed. Shar had almost forgotten how great her bed felt. She would admit to anyone that traveling had its perks, but when it was all said and done, there is truly no place like home.

"Ummm, just for a minute," she murmured. Little did she know, that very minute would take her well into the evening.

"Hey Galvi man, it's your bro. I know I told you I was handling the meetings in Miami but you could at least call a brother and see how things are going. Dang. Nah, I'm just kidding ya. But on the real, mom said she's been trying to reach you but she keeps getting your voicemail. She's home and she wants to see us Sunday. It would be their 45th anniversary man. Anyway call me. I know all is well but call me anyway. Yo."

"Are you ready Mr. E?" asked the pilot.

"Almost, let me make one more call."

"Hello."

"Hey baby, it's Ezekiel."

Trying to sound awake, Shar perked up a little.

"Hey how are you?"

"I'm great, but I'm going to be even better when I see you."

"Is that so?"

"Well yes indeed and that's going to be really soon."

"Well I can't wait to make you feel better than great. Is your business done in Miami?"

"It certainly is and I'm about to board my plane and head your way."

Shar sat up in the bed and glanced at her phone to check the time. A little startled by how much time had passed since she got home, she quickly replied, "That's great, do you need me to come get you from the airport?"

"No, no, no, you've been doing enough. I should be there in about an hour and I'll get a car then. All I need you to do is text me your address."

"Got it. See you soon."

"See you soon."

Shar exhaled and allowed herself to fall back dreamingly on her bed. If she didn't know any better, she would've sworn she landed on the clouds. She closed her eyes and smiled, thinking about how great she felt when Ezekiel was in her presence. She opened her eyes, stared upward to the ceiling and gave thanks to God for everything in her life including the pain she's endured. She understood that without the pain, she could never truly appreciate the joy.

Shar enjoyed that moment a little while longer until it dawned on he that Ezekiel would be there in less than an hour now. She almost panicked but she kept her cool. She calmly got out of bed, went to the kitchen and began preparing some chicken and shrimp for dinner.

"I'll have this ready in case he wants a home cooked meal. Maybe he'll help with the finishing touches."

She seasoned the meat and shrimp, chopped some onions and peppers and heated a pan with a little grapeseed oil. While the onions and peppers simmered in the pan, Shar brought some water to a boil with a little butter and sea salt in a separate pot, and added some linguini. She left the kitchen temporarily to pull out one of her patterned maxi dresses and a matching bra and panty set. She showered the items with a little Chanel No. 5 and went back to the kitchen to stir the noodles. She couldn't resist tasting a noodle, she usually timed them to perfection.

She removed the pot from the heated element and added the chicken to the pan.

"Mmmmmm," said Shar as she breathed in the aroma from the spices as she stirred the chicken.

She turned the heat down a little, covered the pan and went back to her room to text Ezekiel before taking a shower.

"Okay, that's done, time to freshen up a bit."

Shar turned the shower on nice and hot like she liked it, secured her hair in her shower cap and scrubbed her body clean with her avocado soap. She lathered her body several times and let the hot pulsating water rinse her well. She would stay in the shower all night if she could, but time was of the essence tonight. She washed her face and rinsed for the final time before stepping out of the shower to dry off. The bathroom was so steamy, she had to open the door and wipe the basin mirror off with a towel. She brushed her teeth, rinsed her mouth and smiled before she blew herself a kiss. She went into the bedroom, got her shea butter oil off the dresser and sat at the foot of her bed.

"Something smells great," she thought just as she was about to squeeze the oil into her hands.

"Oh shoot, the chicken!"

Shar got up and went to the kitchen to check on the chicken, it looked great. She added more peppers and onions before stirring it a bit then she added the shrimp and a little more oil. Shar pulled out a bag of garlic knots from the freezer, placed five on a baker's pan and pre-heated the oven to 375 degrees. She drained the pasta and took everything in. She was good and she knew it. The chicken and shrimp were cooking nice and slow and the aroma was so amazing, she decided to open her patio door and share it with her neighbors.

On her way back to the kitchen, her phone started ringing. She went into the bedroom to answer it; it was Ezekiel.

"Hello."

"Hey Shar, it's me. I got your text and I should be there in about 20 minutes or so."

"Great. How was your flight?"

"I can't complain. God got us here safe and sound. It was quite smooth."

"Glad to hear it, I can't wait to see you."

"Likewise. Have you eaten yet?"

"Not yet. I actually was cooking some chicken and shrimp pasta."

"That sounds good. I hope you didn't go through a lot to make it. We could have gone out to eat or ordered in."

"No, no. It was no trouble at all. I'd missed being home cooking actually. I hope you like it. You aren't allergic to anything are you?"

"Nah, baby the only thing I'm allergic to is not eating good food, but I know I don't have to worry about not liking anything you make."

"Oh God, the pressure is on now."

"No worries," said Ezekiel followed by a little laughter.

"We'll see, let me finish getting ready. Call me if you need me."

"Will do, see you in a few."

"Okay."

While Shar was talking she stirred the chicken and shrimp, added the rest of the onions and peppers and placed the bread in the oven.

She went back to her room and finished getting ready. She thought about putting on a little eye make-up but decided not to. She wanted Ezekiel to see her natural beauty tonight; dabbing on a little oil on her lips for gloss and letting her hair be free from restraints.

She washed her hands and glanced at herself in the mirror before going back to the kitchen. The garlic knots smelled delicious and they were golden brown; time was truly on her side tonight. She was almost done. All she had to do was just add the noodles to the pan, stir the contents and reduce the heat.

The aroma tempted Shar to have a taste before Ezekiel arrived but instead she opted for fresh breath upon his arrival. She began to set the table and just as she reached into the cabinet to get some wine glasses, there was a repeated knock at the door. She placed the glasses on the table and took a bottle of Vintage San Sebastian from the wine cooler before approaching the door. Before she could ask who is it, the knocks were repeated.

"Who is it?"

"Open the door and find out beautiful."

"I'm sorry you're going to have to come better than that mister."

She knew it was Ezekiel before she looked out the peep hole and seeing a glimpse of him from the side; she'd recognized that deep sexy voice anywhere. She simply enjoyed the illusion of suspense.

"That's what I'm talking about, it's me Ezekiel."

Shar removed the chain from her door and unlocked it.

"Hi there, you made it. Come in."

"Yes, I told you I was coming. I couldn't miss seeing you before I went home," he said as he leaned in to kiss her on the cheek.

"These are for you."

"Awww, thank you. They are beautiful."

"A beautiful Amaryllis, for a beautiful woman."

"They are gorgeous. Thank you."

"You're welcome. You look great."

Shar smiled with flowers cradled in her arms and the wine bottle in her right hand. She returned the compliment and sat the wine down on the table.

"You have impeccable timing. I just took the bread out of the oven and the pasta is ready to be served. Make yourself at home."

Ezekiel rubbed his stomach with anticipation.

"Well it smells great. I'm ready if you are. Can I help you with anything?"

"Sure. I could use a vase off the shelf for my beautiful flowers and you can open the wine. The opener is on the table."

"On it. What kind of wine is this anyway?" he asked as he picked up the bottle.

"San Sebastian, I hope you like it."

"I'm sure I will."

He popped the cork and poured the wine in their glasses and Shar brought the bread and pasta to the table.

"Tell me when," said Shar as she filled his plate with pasta.

"That's plenty," he said after the third scoop.

"Would you like some cheese or anything else?"

"Nothing at all, it looks great. You totally outdid yourself."

He leaned over to kiss Shar on the lips this time and she tried to stop herself from blushing, but couldn't.

"Stop it, you haven't tasted it yet," she said as she put a few scoops on her plate.

"Have some bread, they're garlic knots."

"But of course," he said reaching in the bowl.

Shar helped herself to a piece of bread as well and invited Ezekiel to do the honors of blessing the meal. Ezekiel took Shar's hand in his and began, "Dear Father. Thank you for this meal that we are about to receive. Please bless the beautiful hands that prepared it and bless those who are less fortunate. Father, thank you for blessing me with an opportunity to meet such a beautifully, spirited person. With your guidance, let us continue to be a blessing for each other. In your name we pray. Amen."

"Amen."

They picked up their forks, twirled the pasta around and took the first bite.

"Lord, I hope he likes it," Shar thought.

Ezekiel closed his eyes as he chewed.

"Wow, this is really good. Look at you."

"You like it?"

"I love it."

Shar sighed with relief.

"I'm glad you like it."

"I kinda' knew I would, I mean, I wasn't worried."

"Yeah right," said Shar before taking a sip of wine.

"Now that I know you can cook, it's on and popping now."

"What do you mean?"

"I'm just saying when I want something good to eat, I know I don't have to wait and go to my mom's house."

"Oh is that right?"

"Well, I hope that's the case."

"You know Florida is quite a distance from New York, just saying," said Shar with a little laughter.

"Hey, let me worry about that and don't crush my wishful thinking now."

"Okay, darling, whenever you want my cooking, I got you."

"That's more like it. So how's your family? Have you talked to your parents since you've been home?"

"Not since I got home. I mean I did let them know I made it home safely. When I left, they were both doing fine and everything seemed to be in place."

"That's wonderful. I know he gave you quite a scare."

"Yes he did. I'm glad you were there for me. I don't know what…"

Ezekiel grabbed her hand and Shar stopped talking mid-sentence.

"How's your mom?" asked Shar.

"She's great actually. I talked to her today. She wants Galvi and I to come over on Sunday for dinner."

"That should be nice."

"Yeah, that day marks 45 years her and my pops would have been together."

"Wow."

"Speaking of that, I tried to call Galvi and let him know but I haven't been able to reach him."

"Come to think of it I haven't heard from Maniya either. I wonder if they've been occupying each other's time."

"It's possible. I know I wish I could be occupying more of your time."

"Is that so?"

"Yes it is so my lady."

"Well we'll have to see about that won't we?"

They were both grinning from ear to ear and Shar was feeling extra good as she sipped on her wine and finished eating.

Ezekiel topped their glasses off again and helped himself to another knot.

"I like this wine. It has a nice taste to it."

"Yeah, I fell in love with it when I went to the winery in St. Augustine."

"It was an excellent choice. I don't know about you but I'm stuffed."

"Me too."

"Everything was great, thank you so much."

"It was my pleasure, I'm glad you enjoyed it."

Ezekiel got up and started to clear the table.

"No, I got it. You can go in the living room and find something for us to watch while our food digests."

"Don't be silly. I'm going to help you put things away."

"Well if you insist, I won't turn away a helping hand."

They cleared the table, washed the dishes and stored the leftovers before finding themselves a cozy spot on the sofa. They nestled closely while channel surfing and continued enjoying each other's company.

Shar couldn't quite wrap her head around a time that she felt this comfortable with a man. There was something present with Ezekiel that she'd been deprived of and she doesn't want to let it go. Wouldn't you know Ezekiel was running the same thoughts through his mind about her!

They comforted each other throughout the night engaging in conversation and caressing each other mentally and physically for hours on end. In the midst of it all, Shar remembered that the patio door was still open. She reluctantly removed herself from Ezekiel's arms to get up and close it.

"What's wrong?"

"Nothing, I just need to close the patio door before I forget."

She stepped away a few feet, but the way he anticipated her return would have made you think she'd travelled miles.

"Come here," he said to her as he guided Shar to straddle him on the sofa. He encased her face gently with his hands and bit her bottom lip softly which led to a passionate kissing fest.

Shar closed her eyes and let the passion take her away. With every stroke of Ezekiel's strong hands caressing her back, she felt a sensation that prompted seductive moans and sensual movements.

"What are you trying to do to me?" she asked.

"Love you if you let me.'

"I'm scared. I'm living here and you're in New York."

"Let me worry about the distance, I can take care of that."

"How?"

"My focus is you, we will be there for each other and although we can't see each other every day physically, we can Facetime and talk."

Amid talking, their tongues and lips joining forces, the Music Choice button was pressed on the remote control and Maxi Priest's song "Every Little Thing" was on.

Every time she heard that song she thought of how good it would feel to have someone feel that way about her and mean it.

"Wow," she thought, "what are the odds?"

Captivated by his touch, kisses on her neck and this song coming on out of nowhere, she failed to respond to Ezekiel's comment.

"So how about giving us a chance," reiterated Ezekiel?

Shar had given other men a try that couldn't hold a light to Ezekiel so she decided to lay her heart on the table.

The music from the television began to fade as they created their own melody using their bodies as instruments. Everything was in tune as if they'd practiced days on end for hours at a time. They were in sync, not a single note was off key.

As their bodies touched and shifted about the sofa and living room floor, passion grew intensely.

"No regrets," said Ezekiel as he looked into Shar's eyes.

"No regrets," she replied as her eyes rolled to the back of her head.

Their moment of ecstasy was followed by a warm bubble bath together and cuddling. The next morning they had breakfast in bed followed by a little work from home to keep them grounded. They moved around like little bees taking a little time here and there to give each other kisses along the way. Later in the day, they turned off their phones and drove down to St. Augustine to have a late lunch and a nice stroll on the beach.

It was such a beautiful and relaxing atmosphere; they decided to stay a little longer. The sun was setting and the city's night lights were coming on. Shar thought they were walking down the sidewalks of the old city aimlessly; she had no clue that Ezekiel had scheduled something for them to do when they were in the restaurant.

"This is really nice but I know we have stayed longer than we planned. We can leave when you're ready," said Shar.

"Oh no, I'm fine. I'm enjoying every moment of this, besides there's one more thing we have to do before we go."

"What's that?"

When they turned the corner, there was a carriage with two white horses in front.

"After you my lady," said Ezekiel as he extended his hand to help her get in the carriage.

Shar looked at him with a glimmer in her eyes and smiled.

"Awww. This is so beautiful."

The coachman stood to the side of the carriage tipping his hat and extending his hand to assist Shar as well. When Ezekiel entered the carriage with Shar, the coachman gave him two dozen of long-stemmed pink roses in which he presented to Shar.

"Thank you babe," she said before giving him a big kiss on the lips.

"Did I surprise you?"

"I had no clue! You're good! I've always wanted to go on a carriage ride too."

The coachman began to tour the city with Ezekiel and Shar enjoying the scenery under the moonlit sky.

They couldn't have asked for a better way to close the day there.

The next morning Shar and Ezekiel said their good-byes before he left for the airport. He assured her that they would be seeing each other soon and she would not regret giving him a chance. When she closed the door behind him, she was missing him already. It felt good to have a man around the house for a change.

Shar thought it was odd that her phone hadn't made a noise in a whole day, so she decided to check it out.

"No wonder I haven't received any calls," she said, "it's still off."

When she turned her phone on she had messages from her parents and Maniya. Her parents were fine, they were just checking on her and Maniya wanted to catch up because it had been a while since they talked. Shar decided to take a shower before calling them back. She took in a deep breath, still able to smell Ezekiel's cologne in her room and smiled from ear to ear as she made her way to the shower.

Chapter 20

Friday Night

Ezekiel had a safe flight home and when he arrived, he retrieved messages from his phone which included one from Galvi.

"Hey bro, I got your message. I'll see you and mom Sunday. Sorry I missed you earlier but I was handling a game changing situation. Give you more details when I see you."

"I wonder, what that's all about," thought Ezekiel.

He knew what or better yet, who, was on his mind. So he gave in to unwinding after a day of traveling and spent the rest of his night thinking about the time he and Shar shared together.

Chapter 21

In the Same Moment

"Where have you been 'Ms. Lady'," asked Shar?

"If I told you, you wouldn't believe me."

"Try me."

"Guess who popped up at my place a few days ago."

"Who?"

"Deran."

"Get out."

"No really, and he had the nerve to try to get violent with me. He told me he wasn't letting me go that easily and all kinds of stuff."

"No. What happened?"

"Galvi happened honey. He came through at the right time and shut Deran down."

"What?"

"Yes ma'am. Needless to say, we are involved now and I'll spare you the rest of the details," said Maniya joyfully.

"Wow, I like how you did that. I let you slide for now because it seems like we both had some craziness going on but it ended with a great thrill. I decided to give Ezekiel a try too."

"Ohhhh, you did?!" screamed Maniya.

"I did and it feels great. He just left to go back to New York this morning."

"Whattt? Get it Shar."

"I'm glad we got together in New York when we did our girl vacation."

"I know, I wouldn't change a thing."

"What are we going to do next year though?"

"What do you mean? Did you forget about Tahiti?"

"That's right, it's time for us to go out of the country and Tahiti was our top choice like three years ago, right?"

"Yep."

"Wow and it's almost here. Well if we keep up our relationships it might turn into a couples retreat."

"Hey I'm down for that."

"How is everything else going with mom and pops?"

"Oh they are great, you have to come down and see them one weekend."

"I will definitely. Maybe Galvi and Ezekiel can steal away some time too so we can all experience some Florida fun."

"That would be great. Well I'm not going to hold you up any longer. See you soon and let's get ready for Tahiti, it will be June before you know it."

"I know right, see you soon."

Chapter 22

Sunday evening

Sunday came and Ezekiel and Galvi's mom could not have been more pleased with her sons. They both looked great and things were going well for them in all areas of their life. Galvi shocked them both when he announced he had a love interest.

"I'm proud of you bro, I knew you had it in you."

"E, get out of here man."

"Yeah leave your brother alone, let's just pray it lasts."

They all laughed and finished their meal together.

Meanwhile, the smiles and smirks on their faces were evidence that their imagination was going wild with the possibilities of what the future held in store for them.

Chapter 23

One Year Later

"Is it me or does it seem like it was yesterday that we confirmed our trip to Tahiti?"

"I know, those seven months just flew by," said Shar as they waited to receive their welcoming flower lei at the Manava Suite Resort.

"It's so captivating here; the pictures don't do it justice."

"And that's crazy because the pictures are breathtaking."

They checked into the resort, got situated and went for a walk on the beach.

"I wish the guys could have come, they were excited about coming."

"I know, but that's how business goes sometimes. When there are fires, you got to put them out. Besides, we did all manage to get together a few times in Florida and New York."

"You're right. Well we'll have fun for them and tell them all about it."

"They're probably hating life right now back in the states."

"Alright, enough about them, let's enjoy this beautiful island. Is that a bar over there?"

"It sure is."

The girls went over to the beach bar and ordered drinks.

"Mmmm, this is great."

"Yes ma'am. This is what life is about Shar. Look at us, we couldn't imagine this as kids, but our "in due time" has made its way to our present."

The ladies stopped walking and took in the scenery. The ocean was magnetic, purely intoxicating. Some people were running along the shore and others were reclined enjoying the sunrays and the nice breeze. The ladies did a 360 degree turn and the ocean grabbed their attention once more. They blocked out all movement around them; it was as if the ocean had them in a trance.

"Shar pinch me because I think I'm dreaming."

"It's not a dream," said a masculine raspy voice from behind.

Shar and Maniya turned around to find Ezekiel and Galvi towering over them shirtless and barefoot with ivory linen pants on.

"You ladies didn't really think we were going to miss this trip, did you?" asked Ezekiel.

They were so excited to see them, that they dropped their glasses and gave them hugs and kisses. Being the gentlemen that they are, they bent down to pick up the glasses. But, instead of standing up right away, they both stayed on a bended knee and reached into their pockets.

Shar and Maniya looked at each other and down at their men.

"Baby what are you doing?" asked Shar with tears in her eyes.

Maniya was unable to speak but tears were rolling down her face. Ezekiel and Galvi took their hands out of their pockets with little blue boxes in tow. They each opened the box and revealed two gorgeous princess cut diamond rings.

"Shar," said Ezekiel.

"Maniya," said Galvi.

Both girls said yes simultaneously.

"Will you marry me?" asked the men in unison.

The ladies nodded yes without hesitation. Shar and Maniya looked at each other for a brief moment with tears flowing down their faces like raindrops. Their dresses were blowing in the breeze and the ocean blue created a perfect backdrop curtain now more than ever. The "in due time" they'd always waited for was truly here and now.

THE END

Message From The Author

Thank you so much for purchasing this book. I hope you enjoyed it. There's a lot of love in these pages and I have more to give. Are you ready for the sequel?

Contact Me:
jenaelashay@gmail.com

IN DUE TIME IS AVAILABLE ON AMAZON

Jenae LaShay lives in Florida. She is a graduate of the University of North Florida. She has a passion for writing and public speaking.

Made in the USA
Middletown, DE
31 March 2025

73428339R00152